STUNT TARGET

Frank raced the red Porsche across the smooth green lawn. No sabotage here, he thought as the restraining cable caught, stopping the car.

"That's a wrap," the director said, nodding happily. "But let's take one more for insurance. Action!"

Frank floored the gas pedal and aimed the car for the house. Right on cue, Janet came out the door and onto the porch. She pretended to freeze in horror.

The Porsche reached the foot of the steps, and Frank waited for the cable's jerk. It didn't come!

He stomped on the brakes, but the pedal sank to the floor. The car plunged ahead, smashing into the first brick step. Frank's hands were nearly thrown from the wheel. It took everything he had to fight the out-of-control car.

But even as he battled the steering wheel, the car hurtled up the steps, straight for Janet!

Books in THE HARDY BOYS CASEFILES® Series

Available from ARCHWAY Paperbacks

SCENE OF THE CRIME

FRANKLIN W. DIXON

AN ARCHWAY PAPERBACK
Published by POCKET BOOKS

New York   London   Toronto   Sydney   Tokyo

AN ARCHWAY PAPERBACK *Original*

An Archway Paperback published by
POCKET BOOKS, a division of Simon & Schuster Inc.
1230 Avenue of the Americas, New York, NY 10020

ISBN: 0-671-64687-7

First Archway Paperback printing February 1989

10 9 8 7 6 5 4 3 2 1

Printed in the U.S.A.

IL 7+

Chapter

1

"FRANK AND JOE HARRIS reporting for work."

A burly guard in a jacket that read "Movie Security" blocked the gate to the film set. His eyes moved slowly from the two boys to the list of names on his clipboard. *The Grand Gambit,* a big-budget Hollywood adventure-romance, had a closed set—so closed, it was locked.

The movie was being shot on location in the small, affluent town of Newbridge, three hundred miles south of Frank and Joe's hometown of Bayport. The place was crawling with TV crews and fans. Across the street from the enclosed set, a mob of teenage girls rushed forward to get a better look at the boys in the black van.

Seventeen-year-old Joe Hardy leaned out the window, showing off his broad, muscular shoulders. His blue eyes gleamed as he ran a hand slowly through his blond hair. "They think we're stars," he said, grinning at his dark-haired, eighteen-year-old brother.

Frank Hardy shook his head. "Pull your head back in," he said. "We're just stunt apprentices, remember? *Undercover* apprentices."

Three days earlier the Hardys had had a Hollywood visitor at their home, Sy Osserman, director of *The Grand Gambit*. He arrived just after the family had finished dinner, and fifteen minutes later Fenton Hardy, the boys' famous detective father, asked his sons to join their discussion.

Frank and Joe had seen pictures of Sy Osserman in the newspapers, of course. The director, who specialized in big-budget action films, was about fifty years old, short and squat, with a large bald head. His silk shirt was pink and looked custom-made.

"Perfect!" he said, greeting the boys. "You've got the look, and you're in shape." Mr. Osserman smiled and bobbed his shiny egg head once. "You take your act to the gym. I like to see that in young people."

"Sy is having a problem." Fenton Hardy stepped in to explain to his confused sons. "A series of strange accidents has caused shooting delays on his new film—"

"The Grand Gambit," Joe supplied the title. "I've read about it in the papers."

The movie starred a hot new star, brash,

twenty-one-year-old Burke Quinn, and his blond, real-life girlfriend, rock singer Kitt Macklin.

The boys' father nodded. "The film has gotten enormous publicity and lots of predictions that it'll be a blockbuster. But now it's badly behind schedule, and every day wasted means hundreds of thousands of dollars lost."

"I've got a lot riding on this project," Sy Osserman said, running a silk handkerchief over his glistening dome. "My last movie was a major flop. If this film doesn't go over, my career will be dead. *Kaput!*"

He gave the thumbs-down sign.

"Every time one of the important action sequences is shot, something goes wrong," Osserman continued. "And I know those accidents are suspicious."

"Sabotage?" Frank asked, his eyebrows raised.

"That's what Sy wants us to find out," Fenton Hardy said.

Frank tried to keep cool, but Joe didn't bother hiding his enthusiasm. School was out for the summer, and he was getting antsy just hanging out. He'd been hoping a new case would come their way.

"When do we start?" Joe asked, grinning.

"This will be a physically demanding assignment." Mr. Hardy studied Joe, then Frank. "I've suggested that you go undercover—as apprentice stuntmen."

Frank nodded. "Great. That way we'll be right in the middle of it."

"I'll arrange for union cards and credentials," Osserman added.

"I'm going to fly out to Hollywood in the morning to do a little investigating at that end," Mr. Hardy explained. He placed a hand on each of his sons' shoulders. "Remember, I want you to be extremely careful. Stunt work is dangerous enough—add some sabotage, and it could be deadly."

Now the Hardys were ready to begin. The security man checked off "Frank and Joe Harris" and stepped aside. Joe gave the girls one last wave as Frank drove the van through the gate.

The entire set was the size of a county fairground. It ran for nearly a mile from the edge of the Garfield mansion, where much of the film was being shot, to the famous Newbridge cliffs. The mansion was not behind the fence the movie crew had constructed. It was set off the road about one hundred feet, and guards were stationed along the front perimeter.

Following signs to the parking area, Frank and Joe drove through much of the lot. Crew people rushed all around them, moving props, electrical equipment, sound booms, lights, and cameras. They passed a couple of outdoor sets—one a replica of a city street, another of a country town. After those came the small buildings and trailers that housed the crew and equipment. And at the far end of the lot were the exclusive stars' quarters.

Sy Osserman was easy to spot. Wherever the director went, a host of assistants followed. Osserman was growling out a list of orders when he noticed Frank and Joe walking toward him.

Instantly his snarl turned to a smile. "Ah, my two new stunters have arrived." The director glanced around. "Where's Ray Wynn?" he shouted to no one in particular. "Tell the old captain I want to see him—pronto."

Seemingly out of nowhere, a thin, wiry man, with hard-edged features on a deeply tanned face, stood before them. He wore baggy old sailor pants and a work shirt. A sea captain's cap covered much of his white hair.

The director introduced Frank and Joe.

"I'm Ray Wynn, stunt captain." He glanced at the Hardys' union cards. The fake credentials passed the captain's inspection.

"Harris brothers, huh?" he mumbled. "You two seem a little young. But I'll see if you can handle the action—because that's what you're going to get, plenty of it."

"That's what we came for," Joe said.

The director left them to go to the next shot.

"Frank, your dark hair matches Burke Quinn's," the captain said. "Suppose you drive for him in the next sequence?"

Wynn led them to the costume trailer. In minutes Frank was fitted with a black tuxedo, and a car was taking him, Joe, and the captain to the Garfield mansion. Ivy covered the three-story brick-front Colonial house, which marked the end of Mansion Row—a half-mile stretch of glamorous homes on ten-acre lots lining the cliff that overlooked the ocean. Back in the 1890s these mansions had turned Newbridge from a sleepy sailing town into the center of high society.

The captain explained that they'd be shooting the scene at the mansion. It was supposed to be night, but it was being shot in daylight with a filter on the camera. Frank would drive a red Porsche across the front lawn toward the house at high speed. Kitt Macklin's stunt double would step out in front of the car to look as if she was going to be plowed down.

"You mean I'm going to drive a car straight at the house?" Frank asked. "Why would I do a crazy thing like that?"

"You've got me," the captain said. "That's what's in the script."

When they arrived, Sy Osserman had just called, "Action." Burke Quinn entered, dressed exactly like Frank, and walked along the front lawn with his arm around Kitt Macklin, who looked beautiful in an exquisite evening gown. He smiled and murmured in her ear.

"It wouldn't take much acting to do *that*," Joe whispered, staring at the beautiful singer.

Sy Osserman and a team of sound and lighting

men kept pace with the actors just three feet off camera. After several takes Sy shouted, "That's a wrap."

Kitt instantly brushed Burke off and huffed away.

Next the crew moved across the lawn, to where the red Porsche was set up. Frank sat behind the wheel and carefully looked over the dash. He tested the clutch and the brakes. Everything seemed right. He was ready. Then he climbed out of the car and sat and waited. Frank had heard there was a lot of hurry-up-and-wait on a movie set, and now he was a victim of it.

Finally, when he thought they'd totally forgotten him, he was called and the car was returned to the set.

"Okay, Frank," the captain said, his eyes glittering. "Time to drive. Don't worry, the cable we've rigged to the rear of the car will stop you in time. I promise."

Frank looked at the mansion, thirty yards away. Standing by the door was a woman, who at first glance looked like Kitt Macklin.

"That's my daughter, Janet," the captain said. "I've raised her to be a top stunter."

Sy Osserman shouted through his megaphone for everyone to clear the area.

"Action!" he bellowed.

Frank threw the car into gear and roared forward. As he approached the house, the front door opened, and Janet Wynn stepped out directly in the car's path.

Sweat poured down Frank's temples as he continued to race toward her. Then, just a couple of feet before the house came a jolt that slammed him deeper into his seat. The cable held as the car screeched to a stop.

"Okay. Not bad," Sy growled. "But let's try this baby again."

Everyone was in place and Frank once more raced the Porsche across the smooth green lawn. This time he felt less worried. No sabotage here, he thought as the cable caught again.

"That's a wrap," Sy said, nodding happily. The fans gathered across the street roared their approval. "But let's take one more for insurance."

Frank put the car in reverse and rolled back to his starting point, awaiting his signal.

"Action!"

Frank floored the gas pedal and aimed the car for the house. Right on cue, Janet came out the door and onto the porch, framed by two heavy wooden pillars. She pretended to freeze in horror.

The Porsche reached the foot of the steps, and Frank waited for the cable's jerk. It didn't come!

He stomped on the brakes, but the pedal didn't respond. It sank mushily to the floor.

The car plunged ahead, smashing into the first brick step. Frank's hands were nearly thrown

8

from the wheel. He didn't dare reach for the emergency brake. It took everything he had to fight the out-of-control car.

But even as he battled the steering wheel, the car hurtled up the steps, straight for Janet!

Chapter

2

FRANK HAULED DESPERATELY on the wheel, sending the sports car into a high-speed swerve straight at the right-hand pillar.

Janet dove left off the porch, then somersaulted onto the grass just as the car crashed. The front end folded up like an accordion as the pillar collapsed, sending the roof of the small porch crashing down. Thick dust rose up all around the Porsche as debris battered the hood and smashed the windshield.

Joe dashed for his brother at full speed. He seized the driver's door and yanked hard.

"Frank!" he yelled. "Are you all right?"

After three heaves, the door screeched open. By now, the rest of the anxious crew had arrived.

"I'm okay, I think," Frank said shakily as Joe helped him out. "Just a little bruised."

The captain leaned over Joe's shoulder. "You were lucky to survive a head-on collision at that speed," he told Frank.

"How's the girl?" Frank asked.

"Fine," she said, coming up behind them.

Up close, Janet Wynn looked less like Kitt Macklin—but she was beautiful like Kitt. She had striking green eyes, long blond hair, and a dazzling smile. And, as her jump had demonstrated, she was athletic. Frank noticed the same glow in her eyes that he'd seen in her father's before the stunt began.

"Thanks for swerving," Janet said with a smile. "It showed me which way to leap."

"There shouldn't have been any reason to leap." The captain clenched his hands as he surveyed the damage to the car. "Not that I blame you, Frank. You did the sensible thing. But this should never have happened."

Frank took a few steps to check out his body and see how bruised he was. "Look at the brakes," he told Joe. "They sank straight to the floor when the cable didn't hold. I was lucky the seat belt held, or I'd have gone through the windshield. What happened to the cable, by the way?"

As members of the crew started to roll the smashed auto off the porch, Wynn answered, "Someone's checking it out."

When the car was on the grass, Joe crawled under it. "I don't think I'm going to find anything, but I should check,'' he called up to Wynn. A moment later he pushed himself back out.

''No good,'' he said. ''That trip up the stairs destroyed the undercarriage. It's just too messed up to give us any ideas.''

''Those brakes were fine.'' They could hear the anger in the captain's voice. ''I checked them out myself. And cables that thick don't just break. If someone didn't tamper with this stunt, I'll trade in my union card.''

''Don't lose your cool.'' Sy Osserman's voice was loud. He'd been the last to walk up, and Frank noticed how shaken up he was.

''We've just had some tough luck, that's all.'' Osserman sounded as if he were trying to convince himself. ''Don't go talking about tampering, Captain. We wouldn't want our reporter friends to get the wrong impression.''

The director's eyes darted over at the Hardys; he was pleading for help.

''Bad luck? I think that crash was the best luck possible. Made a great shot, and we've captured it all on film,'' said a voice behind them.

Together, Frank and Joe turned to the man who'd just joined the conversation. He was tall, with an athlete's build, black hair, a deep tan, and chiseled features. He smiled at them and clapped a heavy hand on Frank's shoulder. Frank winced.

''Great driving, Harris,'' he said. ''I'm Gil Driscoll, top stunt man on this, or any, movie.

Stick close to me, and I'll teach you boys a thing or two. You are brothers, right?''

Joe nodded and noticed someone standing behind Gil Driscoll. Someone Frank and Joe had seen many times before.

Ed Kemble, though he was getting on in years, was still a big star. Frank and Joe had seen most of his adventure films at the Bayport six-plex. Joe, in particular, was a big fan. And here was Joe's hero right in front of him.

Ed Kemble's thick mustache that covered his upper lip was his trademark. His brown hair was close-cropped, as always, and his brown eyes twinkled as he grinned at the boys.

"Wonderful driving, Mr. Harris," Ed said, shaking Frank's hand. "I'm Ed Kemble." He clasped Joe's hand as well and repeated the introduction, as if Joe had never heard of him.

"It's really a pleasure to meet you," Joe said.

"Pleasure's all mine," Ed replied.

He moved off to the side of the smashed porch, and motioned for Frank and Joe to follow.

"I probably wouldn't have thought to shoot for the pillar," he said. "Car stunts are tricky. And I ought to know—I started out in this business as a stunter. Even as a leading man—before I took on this supporting role to help out Sy here—I did all my own stunts."

"Hey, everyone," the captain shouted. "Take a look at this." He held up one end of the safety cable. Frank and Joe joined the rush over to take a look.

"Well, it wasn't cut straight through," Frank determined, examining the tightly wrapped metal strands. "But it does look frayed."

"Maybe the cable gave out after too many takes," Joe said. "It caught the first two times."

"Too many takes?" Sy Osserman slapped his forehead with his palm. He looked at Joe as if to say, "Hey, aren't you working for me?"

"That cable should have caught *every* time," the captain insisted indignantly. "What are the odds of both the cable and the brakes failing? Especially after I checked out the car."

"When did you check out the car?" Kemble asked.

"A couple of hours ago."

Ed Kemble scratched his mustache in thought. "You know, I could have sworn I saw Sy's new star"—he snapped his fingers—"what's his name?"

Gil Driscoll laughed at the idea of Ed forgetting who the film's star was. Frank and Joe exchanged glances. Obviously, Ed wasn't very happy about not being *the* star on the set. Sy Osserman merely heaved a sigh.

"Burke Quinn," the director reminded Ed. "What about him?"

"That's right," Ed said as if he'd just remembered. "Burke Quinn. Why, I saw him just before the shot scooting around the set with his lady friend, in that very car."

"Sure," Gil Driscoll added. "I spotted them, too."

Sy Osserman's jaw hung down. "How did he get permission to take this car?"

A little mousy man in charge of all the vehicles said, "Quinn just took it. Said he didn't need no permission."

"That Quinn's a real funny guy," the captain hissed between his teeth.

Frank pulled Joe a few steps away from the others as the talk turned to Burke Quinn's many antics. The young star had a reputation as a notorious practical joker.

"Let's go have a talk with Mr. Burke Quinn," Frank whispered.

Frank and Joe slowly slipped away from the others. As they departed, a crew of carpenters was arriving to begin repairs on the mansion.

Heading toward the trailers, the Hardys jogged along the cliff top and watched as the cold Atlantic waves broke punishingly over the coastline's huge boulders.

Frank's shoulder throbbed, and each step jarred his body. "Hey, Joe. Slow down," he called out as his brother rushed on ahead.

"Sorry." Joe waited for Frank to catch up.

"What do you think?" Joe asked as Frank joined him. "Was someone out to get you, or was that crash merely an accident?"

15

Frank gave the question some thought. "I doubt Sy Osserman told anyone who we are, or why we're here. So whoever is behind these 'accidents' shouldn't have a reason to harm us."

"But the whole setup worries me," Joe said. "Dad was right. This could turn very deadly."

"Maybe Burke Quinn can give us some answers," Frank said. "But remember, we can't come on like detectives. Let's not raise his suspicions."

"If he fooled with that car, he'll have more to worry about than suspicions," Joe added, his hand balling up into a fist.

Frank shook his head. "Cool it, Joe," he instructed. Too often he'd seen Joe's anger get the better of him.

The actors' trailers were on a small grassy hill away from all the noise. Burke Quinn's was easy to identify. It was a white thirty-footer, with a life-size poster of Quinn plastered to the side. A huge silver star hung on the door. Joe aimed for it as he knocked loudly.

"Who is it?" the Hardys heard the actor call from inside.

"Joe and Frank Harris," Joe shouted through the door.

"Never heard of you," Quinn shouted back. "Go away."

"We're the new stunt apprentices," Frank called out. "We're fans and wondered if we could meet you."

"Not now, I'm relaxing," Quinn said, a hint of laughter in his voice. "A fine actor like me needs his beauty sleep."

An idea came to Joe. "Couldn't you at least give us an autograph, Mr. Quinn?" he asked innocently. "My sister is really hoping for an autographed picture. She has a big crush on you."

The Hardys heard some movement from inside the trailer.

"Door's unlocked, guys," Quinn shouted after a moment. "Come right in."

Joe grinned triumphantly, opened the door—and stepped into a flash of blinding light.

Instinctively, both Hardys dodged back and raised their arms to protect their eyes. But Frank and Joe were still sent reeling by the force of a deafening blast.

Chapter

3

"YOU SHOULD HAVE SEEN the look on your faces!" Burke Quinn stood in the scorched doorway of his trailer, looking down at the boys on the grass. He roared with laughter, slapping his leg.

Frank and Joe staggered to their feet, stunned, wiping dirt from their clothes. Frank's tuxedo was splattered with mud.

"We nearly get blown to bits, and you think it's funny?" Joe looked ready to kill the actor.

"Relax, man," Quinn said nervously. "No harm done. It was all in good fun."

"I ought to knock you silly," Joe said.

"Cool down, Joe." Frank placed a hand on his brother's shoulder and forced his face into a smile. "After all, it was pretty funny."

Joe glared at him. "Are you out of—"

"Hey, Joe," Frank cut him off. "Have a sense of humor." He turned to Quinn. "Mind if we come in and clean up a bit?"

Quinn shrugged. "Sure thing. I promise, no more jokes. You guys have already made my day. That was one of my all-time best."

Frank and Joe went back up the steps. Frank grinned at his host, but Joe couldn't. He could see what Frank was up to, but still couldn't smile.

Inside, the trailer looked more like a penthouse than a camper. Plush beige reclining chairs and a circular couch rested on thick white carpeting. A television, a stereo console, and two large speakers covered one wall. In the back was an antique walnut desk with an executive chair, and beyond that a bedroom.

Frank and Joe walked carefully to the bathroom, making sure not to leave mud on any of the expensive furnishings.

"What *was* that explosion, anyhow?" Frank asked after he and Joe had cleaned up.

"A flash pot," Quinn explained. "A pal in special effects rigged it up for me. They make great fake explosions."

"If it was so fake, how come the trailer's been scorched?" Joe asked, pointing to the door.

"Hey, I can live with that." Burke Quinn waved away the damage. "Seeing you guys jump out of your boots was worth it." Then he jumped off his chair and went to the desk. "I nearly forgot. You wanted autographs, and you've definitely earned them.''

Joe leaned close to Frank, whispering, ''I'd like to tell him what to do with his autograph.''

Smiling, Frank shushed his brother. ''We can't thank you enough,'' he told the actor.

''What did you say your sister's name was?'' Burke Quinn had a pen over one of his pictures.

''Sister?'' Joe repeated. ''Right. Her name is, um—''

''Gertrude,'' Frank finished the sentence for Joe, grinning as Quinn signed the photograph.

''Thanks,'' Frank said enthusiastically. ''Say, did you hear about my accident? I was driving the red Porsche.''

''The red Porsche, you say?'' Quinn's eyes revealed he knew which car Frank meant. ''Smashed up pretty bad?''

''Totaled it,'' Joe said. ''The stop cable didn't hold, and the brakes went out.''

Quinn leaned closer to the Hardys, dropping his voice. ''You guys are new here. Well, you didn't hear it from me, but I'll pass on this warning. Be *careful*. I've got bad vibes about this picture. The stunt team just isn't cutting it. There are constant accidents on this set.''

''Any caused by practical jokes?'' Joe asked.

Quinn gave Joe a cold stare. ''I can see you and I aren't going to be best friends.''

''Hey, Joe just heard a rumor, that's all.'' Frank smiled to ease the tension. ''There's some talk that you were driving the Porsche after it had been checked out.''

"So what if I was?'' Quinn's jaw jutted out. "I took a little spin. I'm the star. I can drive any car I want. And the brakes worked just fine for me. Who told you, anyhow? Kitt Macklin?''

"Doesn't matter.'' Joe shook his head in disgust at Quinn's attitude. "But we heard another rumor—that maybe someone who's into jokes would think it's fun to fool with the brakes before a stunt.''

"I don't need to take this from a pair of apprentices.'' Quinn threw the door wide open. "There's a difference between jokes and killing people. Besides, if I had fooled with the brakes, how would that explain the cable not holding?''

Frank and Joe looked at each other. Quinn was right—the Hardys had no explanation for that. Quickly, they got up to leave.

"Maybe I should have a talk with Osserman about who works on this set,'' Quinn said. "And you can forget about any more autographs for your friends,'' he shouted at their backs.

"Sorry I blew it,'' Joe said as they walked away from the trailer.

"Don't worry,'' Frank told him. "We found out some interesting stuff. Burke Quinn is up for any kind of practical joke, even a dangerous one. And he has the run of the set—''

"And we know that he and Kitt are having some kind of lovers' spat,'' Joe added.

21

"Good deduction." Frank looked down. "Now let me change out of this muddy penguin suit."

Joe laughed. "Wardrobe will love you."

"What can I say? It's been a rough morning." Frank gave Joe a friendly shove. "I'll get back in my own clothes, and then we'll get back where we belong."

"Right. The stuntmen's area," Joe said. "Before we're missed."

The stuntmen had a large makeshift aluminum-sided shed tucked among the rows of equipment trailers in the center of the lot. They entered the building into a lounge area and grabbed a sand-wich each from a platter. To the side of the lounge was a gym, complete with free weights and a Nautilus machine. Behind the lounge was an equipment room and a garage, where cars and motorcycles were fine-tuned, ready for upcoming stunts.

Frank and Joe were surprised to see Ed Kemble hanging out in the stunters' lounge. He was busy swapping stories with Gil Driscoll and two other men. The actor waved Frank and Joe over. "Meet Wesley and Ty."

Wesley was about six foot two, and as broad and tough as a middle linebacker. His head was completely shaved. When he smiled, Frank and Joe saw that all but two of his teeth were missing.

Ty was about an inch taller and slim. The muscles of his forearms bulged even when re-laxed. He had blond hair, a light complexion—

and a sling on his right arm. Frank guessed that he'd also been the victim of a stunt gone sour.

"We've been talking about all the gadgets used in the profession today." Ed picked up a bottle from a table and smashed it over Wesley's head. The glass shattered in a million pieces, and Wesley's eyes glazed over as he hit the floor.

Horrified, Frank and Joe went to help him. But when they grabbed his arms, Wesley grinned and somersaulted to his feet. The others laughed heartily. Even Frank and Joe had to smile.

"Welcome to the trade, guys," Ed said. "It's breakaway glass, as you must know, one of the old-time inventions that are still with us. But nowadays they've added custom-made rubber suits and flame-retardant materials, exploding bullets, and roll bars on all the cars."

Ed shook his head in wonder. "Watch what these little darlings do."

From his pocket, Ed took out what appeared to be a small cherry tomato. He brought it to his mouth, then suddenly dropped the tomato to the ground.

Poof! A flash of light was immediately followed by a haze of thick purple smoke. In a moment, the smoke had cleared and Ed was gone!

"Over here, boys," he called out from behind the sofa. "Nice little flash-bang, huh?"

"Knock it off, Ed." Everyone turned as the captain leaned into the room from the side door.

"I'm trying to prepare Janet for the next stunt. So stop playing with the equipment."

The captain spotted Frank and Joe, and his gruff manner disappeared. "So there you two are. Follow me, I want you to see this setup."

Joe smiled and waved at Ed Kemble as they followed the captain into the garage. A half-dozen men and women were working on two sports cars, a pickup truck, and two motorcycles.

Frank and Joe overheard one mechanic say, "It's those actors," as they passed. "They don't care about anything. They're totally unprofessional." The man was working on the engine of a truck. "Burke, Kitt—even Ed Kemble," he went on. "They're all making us look bad."

"Yeah," the other agreed, "the set's just a playground for them. And if the stunts go wrong, it's an excuse for them if this movie bombs."

"Sy doesn't know what he's doing. He's not in control," said a woman who was tuning up a motorcycle.

Frank and Joe nodded thoughtfully. The accidents were the talk of the crew, and clearly, everyone was under suspicion.

"Cut the chatter," the captain shouted. "Let's keep our minds on our work."

A motorcycle engine revved by the open garage door. Janet Wynn was astride the chopper, wearing a tight, black-leather motorcycle suit. She smiled at Frank, Joe, and her father as they approached.

"Everything checks out, Dad," she said. "I'm ready to go."

The Hardys followed as Janet and the captain rolled the motorcycle outside to a short strip of road that had been laid just for the film. A thick wooden fence was rigged at the end of the road, blocking it. "The fence will be on fire as Janet rides the motorcycle straight through," the captain told Frank and Joe. "It's a breakaway wood frame—it'll be like riding through paper."

Sy Osserman and the crew were already in place. Sy nodded slightly at Frank and Joe, then took his seat behind the camera. Frank noticed that the director had his fingers crossed.

Off to the side, sitting on a canvas director's chair with her name stenciled across the back, was Kitt Macklin. She also was wearing a black motorcycle outfit. Just then she seemed more interested in combing out her long, silky blond hair than in the action.

Kitt looked up and caught Joe staring at her.

"Hello, there," she said in a sexy voice. "I haven't seen you before."

"Joe Harris." He held out his hand. "I'm just a stunt apprentice."

"Actors bore me," Kitt said, smiling into Joe's eyes. "I like men of action."

"Okay," Sy Osserman said. "Let's roll."

Janet put on her motorcycle helmet, straddled the bike, and revved the engine twice. She gave a thumbs-up sign.

At that moment a special-effects person carried a torch over to the wooden fence. He touched one board, and the whole fence burst into flame. There was no time to lose. The crew had only one take to get the shot—or rebuild the fence.

"Action!" the director growled.

Janet roared off. She picked up speed and leaned back, pulling her front wheel off the ground. For fifteen feet she rode out the "wheelie." Frank, an expert rider himself, marveled at her control.

The front wheel touched down, and Janet ducked her head, preparing to crash through the burning barricade—but the wood didn't give.

Janet hit hard. The bike flew out from under her.

She pinwheeled on the ground, a human fireball.

Chapter

4

EVERYONE STOOD FROZEN, staring at the flames licking at Janet.

But Frank was already moving, scooping up blankets left out on a nearby chair for emergencies. He pushed past the crew to Janet, who was silent and not moving.

Joe joined Frank, and together they covered Janet with blankets, to smother the last of the flames. Finally they removed Janet's helmet, and she stirred and groaned.

"Janet! Janet!" The captain's voice was tight as he dropped to his knees beside his daughter. "Are you all right?"

Janet nodded. "Fine," she managed. "Just a bit out of it."

"What about burns?" Joe kept the blankets tight around her. "We'd better get a doctor."

"I'm fine." She grinned up at him. "My suit is made out of Nomex. It's flame retardant. This isn't the first time it's saved my life."

Frank and Joe helped Janet up and led her back from the still-blazing fence. "It's my own fault," she said. "A good stunter always scoops out the whole gag from beginning to end. I forgot to check the fence."

"Well, we can forget that now," Frank said, staring at the flames.

"I should have looked it over," the captain said. "I know on *this* set nothing goes as planned." He turned and glared at Sy Osserman.

"Don't look at me," the director said defensively. "I'm sorry about this accident, but checking that fence wasn't my job."

The captain stomped over to Osserman. "Yeah? Your job is to call *all* the shots around here. Last week Ty nearly had his arm chopped off. This morning Frank and Janet almost got killed. Now she nearly gets burned alive."

The captain looked away—and for a moment he seemed very old. Then his deep brown eyes flashed back and peered sharply into Osserman's. "I know there's sabotage on this set. You know it, too. If we don't find out who's behind it, someone's going to get hurt—bad."

He pulled off his cap and ran a hand through his white hair. "When that happens, you won't be able to keep it quiet anymore," he said in a low growl.

Sy Osserman opened his mouth, but the captain had already turned and was striding away. The director headed in the opposite direction with Frank following him. "The captain is right," he said in a low voice. "Sabotage is the only possible explanation."

Osserman glowered at Frank.

"You thought so yourself," Frank added. "That's why you hired my father, isn't it?"

"I hired your father and you two boys to get *proof*," Osserman said. "Hard evidence."

"Will getting someone killed convince you?" Frank retorted. "I know there'll be more accidents before we get to the bottom of this."

"So what's your point?" Osserman asked.

"I think all filming should temporarily shut down," Frank told him.

The director thrust his moonlike face close to Frank's, his eyes wide in disbelief. "Sure," Osserman said half hysterically. "We'll shut down, send everybody home. The investors and the studio will love that. What do I tell them? Frank Hardy suspects sabotage, so you're out thirty million dollars? No proof yet, but Frank Hardy *suspects*. That'll go over real big."

His right eye twitched. "Tell you what—I'll keep shooting and you keep investigating."

Frank watched as Osserman stormed off. "What was that all about?" Joe asked, when Frank rejoined him and Janet.

"I told him the captain was right," Frank said. "And I asked him to shut down the set."

Joe made a face and shook his head. "Fat chance, right?"

"Right or not," Janet told the Hardys, "Dad shouldn't have shouted at Osserman."

"Well, watching his daughter catch fire probably shook him up," Joe said.

Janet nodded. "More than you know." She started off with the boys flanking her on either side.

"Stunting is a family tradition," she said. "My grandparents were pioneers in the business. And my mom was a top pro."

"Really?" Frank's eyebrows rose. "Is she retired?"

"No," Janet whispered, her voice catching. "My mom's last stunt was running through a burning building. In those days, safety equipment wasn't nearly as good as it is today. Mom"—her voice broke—"my mother never made it out of the flames."

Joe shuddered. He'd seen his girlfriend, Iola, disappear in a flaming fireball, from a terrorist bomb meant for him.

Janet went on, "I was just a kid. When I have to do a fire stunt, I put the tragedy out of my mind."

They were silent then, each lost in individual thought. Finally Frank broke the silence. He looked from Janet to Joe. "I'll tell you what I'm thinking," he said. "If Osserman won't take this sabotage seriously, maybe his stars will."

After leaving Janet at her trailer, Frank and Joe went looking for Ed Kemble. They found him sitting on a deck chair in front of his trailer, holding a reflector to improve his already dark tan.

"Grab a chair, guys," he said. "Cop some rays beside the old star."

Frank and Joe pulled up two chairs on either side of Ed. The actor's eyes were closed, and he hummed an old cowboy song. Joe recognized it as the theme of an early Ed Kemble movie.

"Janet Wynn just had another accident on the set," Frank began.

Ed opened one eye. "No! That's something. The girl really knows her craft, too."

"She's a great stunt woman," Joe said. "But she almost got barbecued."

"Two accidents in one day. Let's see, five in the past two weeks." Ed calculated, shaking his head. "You heard about Ty almost losing his arm?"

Frank and Joe nodded.

"This film isn't worth it to me. My role is too small—a joke compared to what I used to do. I only took the part as a favor to Sy."

"So you wouldn't mind shutting down production until all the problems are straightened out?" Frank asked.

Ed thought that over, narrowing his eyes. "*Sy* would mind. But it's all right with me. In fact, it's great. Safety first is my motto."

He smiled at Frank and Joe. "I think I'll suggest it to Sy in the morning."

Leaving Kemble, the Hardys split up to tackle the two young stars separately. Frank didn't think Burke Quinn would enjoy seeing Joe again. And Joe knew Kitt Macklin would give him a warm reception.

"My natural charm," he told Frank. "Girls understand me. They go for men of action."

"Uh-huh." Frank shook his head doubtfully. "Just don't overplay it, Romeo."

Frank was especially careful when he knocked on Burke Quinn's trailer door. The actor answered immediately, pulling the door wide open. To Frank's surprise, nothing exploded.

Frank could tell Burke Quinn was disappointed to see him—he seemed to be waiting for someone else. Still, the actor invited him in. Frank filled him in on the latest accident.

"Janet was hurt?" Quinn's face showed real concern as he went to the phone. "I'll send her a dozen roses. That'll make her feel better."

He was rude when he called a florist and placed an order for the flowers. Then he looked back at Frank and grinned over his shoulder. "She'll appreciate getting roses from a famous actor. What girl wouldn't?" After he hung up, he flopped down on the couch.

"As for the movie," he told Frank, "if you stunt guys say it's too dangerous to shoot, let's not shoot. They can throw away the whole film for all I care. I only took this role because Kitt asked me to. But the movie stinks. I just hope it doesn't ruin my career."

"Who cares about Janet Wynn!" Kitt Macklin shouted when Joe told her about the accident.

Joe noted that Kitt's trailer was just as plush as Burke Quinn's—except Kitt's was completely decorated in pinks and yellows. A Persian cat hopped up on her lap and mewed to be petted. Joe noticed a framed picture of Burke by the windowsill.

"I may not care about her, but I'm with you all the way," she said, stroking the cat. "Shut down the film. I'm beginning not to like it anyhow."

"Why not?" Joe asked.

"I just don't. That's all." Kitt shrugged as if she didn't need a reason. "I was the one who got Burke his role. Did you know that?"

"No, I didn't." Joe could have said he suspected as much. But he kept his thoughts to himself.

Kitt's expression turned to a pout. "And now all he ever talks about is Janet Wynn!"

Frank and Joe met at the parking lot and compared notes. "Strange that none of the three stars cares about the movie one way or the other,'' Frank said, sliding behind the wheel of their van.

"Especially when you think of all the money they're earning," Joe added.

"Dad will be interested to hear about this," Frank said, looking at his watch. "His call will come through about ten. That gives us time for a good dinner."

But the only inexpensive restaurant in town was an old burger joint on Newbridge's main street. When they finished, Frank and Joe rode the five miles to a motel, where Sy Osserman had reserved a room for them.

"Just like the place in *Motel Massacre*," Joe joked, after seeing the run-down and shabby motel.

"Thanks. I feel a whole lot better now," Frank said.

Fenton Hardy's phone call came through exactly at ten. *The Grand Gambit* is the hot topic in Hollywood," he said. "At first, everyone in the business was interested in the project, but now they're all trying to bail out."

Frank and Joe told their father of the day's mishaps, and of their talks with the three stars.

"Be very careful around Burke Quinn," Fenton warned. "He's done worse than practical jokes in his life."

"What do you mean, Dad?" Frank asked.

"He's the star of my background checks,"

Fenton said. "Before he became a famous actor, he was just plain Bob Quentin."

"That's interesting," Frank said.

"Oh, we haven't gotten to the good part," Fenton Hardy went on. "Bob Quentin spent over a year in the state pen for robbery and assault!"

Chapter

5

THE NEXT MORNING when Frank and Joe drove out to the set, a lineup of cars blocked the front gate. Joe stepped out of the van to see what was causing the delay. Several security guards were checking each car.

"I guess reinforcing security was the least Sy Osserman could do," Joe said.

Fifteen minutes later the van finally pulled up to the main gate. Four tough-looking guards motioned Frank and Joe to get out and hand over their passes. One took their IDs and checked them against a list, while another checked out the front of the van.

"Airport security should be so thorough," Joe said as they drove in to park the van.

Inside, crew members were running in all directions, meticulously preparing for the morning's shots. Equipment was double- and triple-checked to make sure that nothing could possibly go wrong.

Instead of heading straight for the stunt building, Frank and Joe walked past the stars' trailers. "I wonder what they're up to at this time of the morning?" Frank asked.

"Breakfast cooked to order by master chefs," Joe said, grinning. "Or maybe they're grabbing a few more minutes of beauty sleep."

But as they passed Burke Quinn's trailer, Frank and Joe heard loud voices.

"Flowers! How dare you send her flowers!" Kitt Macklin's voice quivered with fury.

The door to Quinn's trailer swung open and the female lead bolted down the steps. Burke Quinn, a half-eaten piece of toast in his hand, stumbled out after her.

"I didn't mean anything," he pleaded. "Janet got hurt; sending flowers was a nice thing to do. That stunt guy, Frank Harris, suggested—"

"Sure, I bet he did," Kitt cut him off.

"Look, I don't even know the girl." Burke Quinn hunched his shoulders as though he knew his lie wouldn't be believed. He turned then and spotted Frank and Joe. Quinn's eyes lit up.

"There's Frank now." He rushed to Frank and pulled him over to Kitt. "Frank, didn't you tell me about Janet's accident?" he asked desperately.

Frank didn't want any part in this fight. "Yes, but—"

Kitt stepped up and grabbed Frank by the collar, as if she were about to haul off and deck him. "But you didn't tell him to send flowers, did you?" she asked accusingly. "And you didn't tell him to talk all day about the great Janet Wynn, did you? And I'm sure you didn't tell him to follow that stunt girl all over the set."

Frank was speechless. He had rarely seen such fire in anyone before. After a moment Kitt pushed him aside.

"No," she concluded. "I didn't think so."

Abruptly, she turned and walked away.

"But, Kitt," Burke Quinn meekly called after her. Then he glared over at Frank. "Well, thanks a lot. I thought guys were supposed to stick up for each other."

Frank held out his open arms, showing there was nothing he could do.

Joe leaned against the end of the trailer, an amused look on his face.

"She has your number, Burke," he said.

Burke Quinn's eyes popped wide. He gritted his teeth and a snarl worked its way up from his throat. He stepped toward Joe.

Frank stopped the actor with a hand firmly placed on Quinn's chest.

"Keep your cool," Frank said. "Joe doesn't mean anything by it."

"I'll teach him to laugh at me!"

Joe placed his hands on his hips. "Sure, Burke," he said. "Try beating me up—maybe you'll rob me, too—as Bob Quentin used to."

Immediately, Quinn's face went pale. He backed away, all the fight gone out of him. "How'd you find out about that?"

"We've got friends in L.A.," Frank replied. "We heard you did a year for assault and battery."

Quinn shrugged and turned away. "The charges were all trumped up. When you're down and out, trying to make it in Hollywood, every cop is out to get you."

"That's not how we heard it," Joe said. "And with everything going wrong on the set, you've got to wonder what Sy Osserman would think if he heard about it, too."

"You wouldn't dare!" Burke Quinn yelled. "I told you yesterday I had nothing to do with those accidents." He waved his arms in frustration, then ran up the steps to his trailer. Turning in the doorway, he glared down at Frank and Joe.

"What I did was nothing," he defended himself. "Lots of actors sometimes have trouble with the law. If you want to know about real trouble, why don't you go talk with Ed Kemble?"

Before either of the Hardys could ask what he meant, Quinn slammed the door in their faces.

Frank turned back to Joe. "I wonder what this Ed Kemble stuff is about?"

Joe shrugged. "He's probably jealous of Ed,

and accusing someone else seems the easiest way out.''

"Could be." Frank shook his head. "Anyhow, that's another lead we'll have to check out."

Back at the stuntmen's headquarters, morale was at an all-time low. No one was working out or practicing for upcoming stunts. Instead, the team sat around listlessly. Wesley looked up from a magazine and nodded at Frank and Joe when they walked in.

The calm was shattered by two booming voices in the next room.

"Don't tell me how to do my job," the captain yelled.

"I don't care about your job," they heard Ed Kemble reply in a level tone. "But I am worried about our safety."

"All you're doing is undermining my authority!" the captain bellowed.

Frank and Joe went over to the doorway and peered in the equipment room. The captain was on his feet. Ed was as calm and as cool as he always appeared in his movies. But the captain's eyes were wide with fury.

"I'm not trying to undermine anyone," Ed stated. "But two near-fatal accidents in one day could be a record."

"Listen, Ed," the captain snarled. "Don't go blaming them on me or my safety procedures. Someone *wanted* them to happen."

Ed Kemble laughed. "Come on, Captain. That's pretty lame."

"It's the truth," the captain said. "And I've got proof."

"Proof?" Ed's tone told the Hardys he was hardly convinced. "I've got no problem, if you've got real proof."

The captain shrugged and glanced away. "It's not much yet. Just a few pieces—"

"Just as I thought," Ed cut him off. "Nothing substantial."

"It will be," the captain assured him. But he was only talking to Ed's back.

"I don't think we should be here now," Frank whispered to Joe. "Let's go."

By then it was too late. The captain had spotted them before they were out the door.

"You two," he commanded. "Don't move."

Frank and Joe froze. The captain walked over, looking them up and down. "Can I tell you boys something?" he said.

The Hardys nodded.

"You went through a lot yesterday, and I think I can trust you." His voice dropped to a whisper. "Now I want to show you something."

He waved them along as he walked over to the far end of the room. "Until I find out more, I don't want either of you to breathe a word of this," he said.

The captain opened a large trunk full of special protective stunt costumes. From the top of the

41

pack he removed the black leather motorcycle jacket Janet had worn the day before.

"Look at this," he said, handing the jacket to Frank.

Frank inspected the jacket. But there didn't seem to be anything odd about it. He handed it to Joe, who shook his head. "Wait a minute." Frank took the jacket back, holding it up to his nose. That was it! An odor coming from the sleeve. He touched it and felt a sticky substance on his fingertips.

"What is this stuff?" Frank inquired.

"The remains of jellied gasoline," the captain said.

"No wonder Janet caught on fire so fast," Joe concluded.

"There's more," the captain added, leading the Hardys from the building. Moments later they were at the fence. It had been left standing, although most of the wood was charred. Still, the fire had been put out before the entire fence was destroyed, and the captain guided Frank and Joe over to the least destroyed area.

"In all our stunts we try to keep the flames confined to one area. But look at this."

Joe ran his finger over the fence and sniffed. "Kerosene."

"Right," the captain said. "But we don't ever use regular kerosene for stunt fires. This part of the fence shouldn't have been on fire at all. Remember, it was supposed to collapse."

"Someone wanted the entire fence to burn down," Frank figured out loud. "That would destroy any evidence of tampering."

The captain pulled his cap down on his head. He smiled at his two apprentices.

"Now you're catching on," he said. "But I think there's more. Whoever set this up had to do it right before the stunt. Otherwise the kerosene would have evaporated." He pointed to where the camera had been. "Now, if the sabotage was done just before the shot—"

Joe's eyes lit up. "You think it might have been captured on film?"

"Why don't we view yesterday's rushes to find out?" Frank suggested.

"That's just what I was thinking," the captain said.

The screening room was in a long building near the director's trailer. It was like a small movie theater, where Sy Osserman and others viewed rushes—scenes that were shot each day.

Rows of soft cushioned seats were set up before the wide screen. A makeshift projection booth was in the back. Through the small open window, the boys could see the large 32-millimeter projector pointed at the white screen.

The captain motioned for Frank and Joe to sit. He went to the back room to locate the reels and thread the film through the projector.

"No popcorn?" Joe joked.

Suddenly the back door opened and the captain

came running down the aisle. There was a worried, desperate look on his face. Frank and Joe saw that his hands were shaking.

"Yesterday's rushes," the captain gasped. "They've disappeared!"

Chapter

6

FRANK AND JOE jumped from their seats and ran back to the projection booth. Frank snatched up a copy of the script, which sat beside the projector, and started riffling through the pages.

"Here's Janet's stunt," he told Joe and the captain. "Scene number two-forty-two."

Shelves full of labeled metal film cans lined one wall. The labels showed the filming date and, since the movie wasn't shot in sequence, gave the scene number from the screenplay.

Joe ran his finger along the canisters of film, reading down the labels. "Reel two-forty-two is definitely missing."

"Hold on." Frank narrowed his eyes and consulted the script. "My crash yesterday into the porch of the Garfield mansion was two-twenty-nine."

"Not here," Joe said, double-checking.

"What! Can't be!" Frantically, the captain began pulling the reels off the shelf.

"The first gunfight's gone." His voice shook. "We're missing a scene at the cliff, and the high dive into the pool is gone as well." Reels spilled onto the floor. "All our hard work—gone."

"Have all the stunt scenes been stolen?" Joe asked.

"All the major ones so far," the captain told him grimly.

"More importantly," Frank added, "all the stunts that were sabotaged have disappeared."

"Quiet," Joe whispered.

They heard someone walking into the screening room. The captain turned off the booth lights as the Hardys waited, their backs against the wall on either side of the doorway. The intruder whistled cheerfully as he pushed open the door.

Frank and Joe both made their move. "Got him!" Joe cried.

The stranger let out a short, frightened scream.

The captain hit the lights, then sagged back onto the stool. "Let him go, Joe," he ordered. "It's only Cal, our projectionist."

Joe released the wiry, blond-haired young man. "Sorry about that. We thought you were our thief," he explained.

But Cal wasn't listening. His eyes were focused on the floor.

"Aaah!" This time his scream was bloodcurdling. "My film! You've destroyed my film!"

Cal dropped to his knees, gathering up as many reels as his arms would hold. Frank, Joe, and the captain looked down at the mess they'd made, then joined Cal on the floor. Before long all the reels were back on the shelves.

Cal counted off the canisters and checked them against a list he kept on his desk. He mopped his forehead with a handkerchief and rechecked the list. "Almost a dozen reels are missing!" He stared accusingly at Frank and Joe.

"We know," Frank said. "We were in here looking for them when you showed up."

"Somebody's taken the stunt scenes—do you know who it might be?" Joe asked.

"Only Sy Osserman, the captain, and the three stars have access to the daily rushes," Cal said. "Anyone else has to get permission."

"Anybody ask in the past few days?" Frank inquired.

Cal considered. A smile came over his face. "Wait a minute. You said the stunt rushes are missing? Ed Kemble always views them."

"Kemble, huh?" the captain snarled.

"Sure," said Cal. "I had them out yesterday to run for him—they looked pretty scary."

"I'll say," Frank murmured.

Frank and Joe convinced Cal and the captain to give them some time locating the missing reels before informing Sy Osserman they'd been stolen.

"If we find the film," Frank explained, "we've got our saboteur."

"I'll give you one hour," the captain said. "Then I have no choice but to tell Mr. Osserman."

Frank and Joe ran off to chase down their first lead. But Ed Kemble's trailer was locked, and the star was nowhere in sight.

"What next?" Joe asked.

" 'Round up the usual suspects,' " Frank said, repeating a famous line from an old movie, *Casablanca*.

Joe grinned. "Burke Quinn is sure going to be happy to see us again."

Quinn wasn't in his trailer either. Frank and Joe did find him just behind the trailers along a path that eventually led out to the Newbridge cliffs. He was dressed in a bathing suit and was carrying a picnic basket. Joe nearly did a double take when he saw Janet Wynn walking beside the actor.

The Hardys kept off the path, staying close to the trailers and buildings where they hoped Quinn wouldn't spot them.

"There you are!"

Burke Quinn stopped dead.

Kitt Macklin stood before him and Janet, arms crossed, her eyes glittering with menace.

"So this is your idea of a picnic lunch." Kitt

looked at her watch a full thirty seconds. "I wait for you for an hour, and where have you been? Out playing with your new girlfriend."

"I just met Janet on the way to your trailer," Quinn explained. "We were only talking."

Kitt's lips were a thin white line. Her hands shook, and tears welled up in her eyes. "I just hope the two of you will be very happy." She choked back a sob.

"Frank! Joe!" Janet Wynn exclaimed, spotting the brothers behind a trailer. "There you are!"

Her expression revealed just how happy she was to see them, to get her out of this jam. Sheepishly, the Hardys joined the others.

Janet took them each by the hand and kissed them both on the cheek. "I'm so glad you finally made it." She turned to Kitt. "These are my dates for lunch," she explained.

Kitt glared doubtfully at the threesome.

"Since we're all here together," Frank said, changing the subject, "I was wondering if any of you heard about the missing film."

"What now?" Quinn asked, exasperated.

"Daily rushes of the stunt scenes are missing." Joe grinned at Quinn. "Sy Osserman will blow his stack when he hears this."

"Anyone know where they might be?" Frank inquired innocently.

Kitt nodded. "Burke must have stolen them."

Burke's mouth opened wide, but no words came out to counter this wild accusation.

Kitt gave him a deadly smile. "He'd do anything for a chance to watch Janet in action." She walked away, leaving a red-faced Burke behind.

Sy Osserman ran a hand over his bald head. He sat in his trailer, glowering at the stunt director and his two undercover detectives.

"They must have been stolen because evidence of sabotage was captured on film," Frank explained. "Our man must have gone back to the screening room last night to grab the goods."

"We'll have to reshoot the stunts," the captain said. His tone suggested that he wasn't happy about the idea.

Osserman stared at him. "Listen, Mr. Stunt Director. Don't think I'm not keeping my eye on you. As far as I'm concerned, this is all your fault." He scowled at the captain. "What are you trying to do, personally ruin my movie?"

The captain glared. "If you recall," he said through gritted teeth, "the rented copter has to be returned today. What are we going to do about reshooting the big helicopter stunt?"

"The helicopter stunt?" Osserman cried out. "The helicopter stunt! We've got to do something."

"Okay." The captain rubbed his palms and got to his feet. The excitement of the stunt had his blood running. "I'll prove to you that I can be trusted. This time, I'll play the Kemble character myself. The camera's far enough away to make it convincing. Frank and Joe can do the fight sequence with me.''

He turned to his two apprentices and smiled. ''You guys up for a good fight?''

Joe winked at Frank and shrugged. ''Anytime, anyplace.''

''The time is now,'' the captain said. ''And the place is on top of a fast-moving train.''

A mile from the Garfield mansion, at the end of the lot, a series of old tracks remained, a relic of the days when Newbridge millionaires rode their private trains to their mansions. Now a freight engine pulled four yellow boxcars around in circles while a helicopter hovered in the sky overhead. It swooped down on the train, then headed back up for another practice run.

As the Hardys changed, the captain explained the scene. Frank and Joe were bad guys, chasing the captain across the top of the boxcars. Frank would catch up to him first. As the train sped along, they'd go through a carefully planned set of punches.

As the captain demonstrated the sequence, Frank shook his head. ''It's more like dancing than fighting.''

''Just make sure you don't go off the side of the train when I knock you down,'' the captain warned. ''You'll get squished.''

Then it was Joe's turn. After another fight, the captain would knock him down as well. Joe frowned. The captain may be tough, he thought, but I wouldn't go down that easy in real life.

Next came the hard part. As the fight with Joe was finishing, the chopper would descend and drop a rope ladder. The captain would make his escape by grabbing the dangling ladder while the copter lifted him off.

"Piece of cake," the captain boasted.

They arrived on the set to find the crew all prepared to shoot. Frank, Joe, and the captain climbed on top of the last boxcar. The engineer started the train slowly around the tracks.

"This isn't so bad if you don't look down," Joe said.

The captain led them on a trial run. The hardest part was jumping from one car to the next. But after the first leap, they had it down pat.

"Action!" Sy Osserman cried.

The captain took off. Frank caught him and they feinted and swung. Most of the time, they didn't even touch each other. From the camera's point of view, though, it would look as if they were taking tremendous punishment. Frank's "knockout blow" was coming. He bent, then crumpled on the roof. He didn't dare look up as Joe started his battle.

Everything went as planned. Joe fell on cue, and the helicopter swooped down. The captain reached up to grab the ladder with one arm, as if he'd been doing it all his life. The chopper pulled him quickly off the top of the train.

"Beautiful," Sy Osserman shouted, and the crew broke out in applause.

But as the crowd was clapping, the rope ladder suddenly unrolled farther. Dangling helplessly from the end, the captain was swinging through the air.

Joe made a grab for him as the copter banked, but the captain was moving too fast. The ladder swung out wide. Then, like a clock pendulum, it swung back—to smash the experienced stunt pro against the side of the train.

Chapter

7

THE CAPTAIN'S EYES rolled back in his head and his grip on the ladder loosened. Joe lunged for the stunter, just as his hands uncurled and he started his fall to the ground. Frank was holding Joe back by the shirt to make sure he didn't leap off into space. But the captain fell, his limp body rolling directly onto the tracks!

"He'll be crushed when the engine comes around again," Joe shouted. "Stop the train!"

But the combined noise of the locomotive and the helicopter taking off again was too loud for the engineer to hear Joe or the shouting crowd. The train continued around the circle of tracks. In no time it had gone halfway around the small loop.

"I'll stop him," Frank said.

He sprinted at full speed, leaping from one car to the next.

Frank's not going to make it, Joe thought, staring at the short distance the train had to travel back to where the captain lay. Sy Osserman and members of the crew were also approaching the tracks, but they, too, could not be on time.

Joe leapt—right off the top of the train. He landed hard inside the circle of tracks. The force of the fall sent him sprawling across the dirt. When he got to his feet, the train was just rounding the final bend.

Joe bolted forward. His left leg ached from the fall, but he didn't think about that then.

Joe heard Frank yelling to him to stop, but he kept going. He reached the captain just as the train came within thirty feet of him. The engineer's jaw hung loose in utter surprise. He blew the whistle and hit the brakes, but the train was moving too fast to stop.

Diving just in front of the train, Joe grabbed the captain under the arms. Unconscious, the wiry stunt director seemed to weigh a ton. Joe shut his eyes and vaulted backward as the train squealed in.

The locomotive stopped about twenty feet farther along. But Joe and the captain were safe and out of the way. "He's alive!" Joe yelled as the crew members came running toward him.

The crew had called for a first-aid team, who ran up with a stretcher. An ambulance's siren sounded in the distance. It was ready to rush the captain to the hospital.

"You okay, Joe?" Frank asked, scrambling down.

"Sure." Joe smiled. "But let me tell you, that was a lot tougher than it looks in those old movies."

A sobbing Janet Wynn had pushed her way through the crowd. "Dad!" she cried, hugging her unconscious father. Finally the ambulance reached them and the medics lifted the captain onto the stretcher. Janet climbed into the ambulance with her father.

"I can't believe this is happening to me," Sy Osserman moaned.

Janet glared down at him from the open ambulance doors. "My father's almost been killed and you're complaining about *your* troubles!"

"But, Janet, honey—"

"I don't care about your closed set," she spoke over him. "My father warned you about sabotage, and you did nothing. Now I'm demanding a police investigation."

Two hours later Janet returned in the back seat of a large blue sedan, driven by a tall, heavy man in his early fifties. He was well dressed in a brown three-piece suit and even wore a matching brown fedora.

Frank and Joe had seen them pull up at the gate and rushed over to ask how the captain was.

"He's still unconscious," Janet told them. "But the doctors are confident that he'll live."

She looked tired and worn out. Her eyes were red from crying, and her blond hair was carelessly pulled back in a ponytail. Her jeans were rumpled now. And over a T-shirt, she wore a satin warm-up jacket with the logo for *The Lost Princess,* an adventure film she had stunted on the year before. Joe thought that was exactly what she looked like, a lost princess, and his heart went out to her.

"This is Chief Archie Fraser, of the Newbridge police," Janet said, introducing the heavy man to Frank and Joe. "I'd like you to tell Mr. Fraser exactly what happened."

"That's all very interesting," Fraser said after the boys finished. He scratched under his chin, where the flesh was loose. "But I'll tell you, I'm not certain what I'm here for. This sounds like an accident to me."

"I'd think like that, too—if this had been the only accident." Janet frowned. "But there have been too many on this set."

Fraser looked at her. "Young lady, before I go any further, I'd like to have a word with Mr. Osserman."

"We'll show you to his trailer," Janet said.

Sy was on the phone when they knocked. But when he saw Janet with the Hardys and the chief of the Newbridge police force, he hung up and invited them in.

"Archie, my man. How are you?" Osserman asked, shaking the policeman's hand.

Joe glanced at Frank. They shared a common thought. It was interesting that the police chief and the director were on such friendly terms.

Fraser plopped down on the sofa and removed his hat. "Tell me about the suspicious accidents this young lady has reported," he said.

"Believe me, Archie," Osserman began, the picture of sincerity, "Ray Wynn's unfortunate fall was an isolated accident. I've already had my own people look into it—"

"What people?" Joe inquired.

"*My* people," the director repeated between clenched teeth. "In fact, we've concluded that the accident was Mr. Wynn's own fault."

"What!" Janet took a step toward the director.

Osserman shook his head sadly. "I'm sorry to say it. The rope ladder was held in place by electronic gears. The captain jerked too hard on the ladder. That made it roll out another length. *He* made the ladder drop down, and that started it swinging."

"That's a lie!" Janet cried.

"Please, dear," Osserman said soothingly. "I know you're upset."

The chief grunted. Frank wasn't sure if that meant Chief Fraser believed the director or not.

Sy Osserman stood and smiled. "There's no trouble we can't handle here, Chief. Let me walk you back to your car."

The policeman stood, and preceded the director out of the trailer. Janet and the Hardys followed closely behind.

"Remember when we first discussed filming in Newbridge?" they heard Osserman say as he walked off with Fraser. "How you, the mayor, and the town council convinced us that this was a great, quiet, out-of-the-way place to shoot?"

"Of course I remember," Fraser murmured.

"Think of the positive aspects for the town," Osserman continued. "There's a special glamour in having a major motion picture shot in your town. Tourists will flock here for years looking at the sights. That is—if the film's a success."

The police chief's lips thinned. "So what's your point, Mr. Osserman?"

"My point is that we don't need negative publicity," Osserman said. "And neither does Newbridge."

The director grinned and slapped Fraser on the back as if they were two old friends in complete agreement. Frank thought Chief Fraser didn't appear so sure.

"All right, Mr. Osserman," he said, opening his car door. "For the time being, we'll keep our distance. But if there's any more trouble . . ."

His words hung in the air as he drove off. Sy Osserman turned and walked back to his trailer with Janet in hot pursuit.

"I don't understand him," Joe said. "He hired

Dad and us to find evidence of sabotage, then he tries to cover it up.''

''He just doesn't want the police involved,'' Frank said. ''Once they start investigating, the press will be all over him.''

Joe nodded. ''So we've got to get the evidence ourselves.''

Frank snapped his fingers. ''And I know just the place to start looking.''

The Newbridge airport was located on the other side of town from the location. It was a small field, mainly used by private jets owned by Newbridge's richer residents. Two hangars stood a half mile from the end of the runway, at the east end of the airport.

''The chopper's got to be in one of those hangars,'' Frank said as he drove beside the runway. ''If the ladder gear was tampered with, the evidence might still be in there.''

In the first hangar, mechanics were busy at work fueling up a small private jet. No sounds came from within the second, and the hangar door was locked. Frank knocked, hoping that someone would answer, but no luck.

''I spotted one window around the side,'' Joe said. ''Maybe we can get in that way.''

The window, which was fitted with a heavy shade, was closed but not locked, and they had no trouble lifting it. Frank climbed in first, Joe following.

Silently, they crept along the wall, making their way across the grayness. Two small prop planes were parked at one end, and a helicopter sat at the other.

"That looks like our chopper," Joe said. "Maybe we should turn on a light. How are we going to find any evidence? It's too dark."

"Sssh!" Frank hissed, a finger to his lips.

They continued making their way toward the helicopter. Suddenly Frank stopped and held his hand out against Joe's chest. They listened for a moment—nothing.

"Just an echo, I guess," Frank said. "All this huge empty space."

He took two more steps.

"Look out!" Joe shouted.

Someone was jumping out of the shadows.

Frank turned—to see a thick wooden board swinging down at his face.

Chapter

8

FRANK LURCHED BACK. The wooden club missed by inches, splintering against the hard concrete floor. As his attacker wound up for another swing, Frank raised his leg and lashed out with a karate kick. The large man bellowed as he doubled over in pain.

From out of the shadows two more thugs closed in on Frank and Joe. The Hardys moved back to back, ready to face attack from any direction.

The hangar was too dark to make out faces, but the Hardys could see their shadowy attackers were big, athletic men, one taller than the other. Both had long switchblades that caught the light.

Joe jumped aside as the taller man lunged in, his knife arm extended. Joe caught the man by the forearm, yanking him forward, and spun him around, pinning the arm behind his back. A painful twist sent the knife skittering on the floor. Then Joe pushed his prisoner into the path of his companion. Both men were down, sprawled on the concrete.

"Sure, don't leave any work for me," Frank said with a smile.

But he spoke too soon. Back on his feet, the first guy with the club slammed at them with what was left of his weapon. Splintered wood swooped wildly about as Joe and Frank dodged back.

Now the other two returned to the battle, and the Hardys lost their advantage. Joe's anger rose as the three attackers closed in.

"I've had enough of this," he roared, throwing a roundhouse right that caught the taller man completely off guard.

The blow landed solidly on the guy's jaw, and down he went. Frank followed suit with a karate chop that caught the shorter man on the side of the head. He dropped, dazed, his knife slipping away.

That left the guy with the club. Only now he wasn't so certain he wanted to fight. He shot a quick glance at his accomplices on the floor. They were shaking their heads, crawling away. Suddenly the man dropped his club and all three made a run for it.

"Come on!" Joe moved in hot pursuit.

They chased the men past the chopper, down to a door at the end of the hangar. The three assailants fled through the door, slamming it in Joe's face just as he reached it.

When Joe and Frank ran out into the sunlight, the men were already pulling away in a black four-door Jaguar. Tires spewed gravel as they turned down the airfield road.

"We'll chase them," Frank said, running ahead of Joe and jumping in behind the wheel of the van. As Joe slammed his door, Frank floored the gas and took off after the Jaguar. "Those guys have no respect for the speed limit," he said as the needle rose past seventy.

The Jaguar roared out the airport gate onto the highway. Frank couldn't close the distance between them.

"I wonder where they're off to," Joe said.

"Don't be surprised if they drive straight to the movie set," Frank replied.

The road was almost free of traffic. Unfortunately, no cops were around to catch the speeding Jaguar. For five minutes Frank kept pace, but couldn't gain any ground.

"They're heading down Mansion Row," Joe said as the Jaguar squealed off the exit ramp.

The Hardys followed seconds later, but the Jaguar was nowhere in sight. Frank sped down Mansion Row, hoping to spot the black car before it turned off onto a side street.

"Over there!" Joe half leaned out the window. The Jaguar was empty, parked at the curb in front of the wooded area separating the Garfield and

Wedmont mansions. A dirt path wound among some trees.

"They must have taken this path," Frank told Joe. "Let's remember the license plate number."

They dashed down the path, keeping an eye open for a possible ambush. But none came, and soon Frank and Joe found themselves on the wide green expanse of the Garfield mansion's back lawn.

"They can't be hiding out there," Joe said, scanning the carefully clipped grass. "Where is the movie crew?"

"They must have shut down for the day—there they are." Frank pointed at the opposite corner of the house as the last of the three assailants rounded it.

The Hardys raced after them, straight across the back lawn. But before they got to the far corner of the house, two uniformed police officers shouted from behind them to stop. They turned to see revolvers drawn and aimed at them.

"Uh-oh," Frank said.

Sirens wailed as two police cars pulled up in front of the house.

"I think we're in trouble," Joe whispered as two more police officers jumped out, revolvers drawn.

Inside the police station, in a swivel chair that was too small for him, Chief Archie Fraser sat behind his gray metal desk.

"Why, it's Frank and Joe Harris." He motioned for them to sit.

"Please inform me why you were running along the back lawn of the Garfield mansion when filming was canceled for today?" Fraser asked. "Planning on robbing the place?"

Frank explained how he and Joe had gone to the airport, and all the events that followed. Fraser folded his hands and listened politely. His mouth turned up to one side, as if he wasn't quite convinced.

"Three thugs. And you say you saw them headed around the corner of the house." He shook his head. "Well, that's impossible."

Joe jumped from his chair. "But it's true! I even memorized their license plate number. The officers must have seen their car—a black Jag." No response from Fraser.

He reeled off the digits as Fraser unenthusiastically jotted them down. Fraser handed the paper to one of his officers and told him to run a check through the state computer.

"Did you see how fast my men were on you when you came across the lawn?" Fraser asked. "You didn't get very close to the house because you tripped the silent alarm."

Frank frowned. "But if we tripped the alarm, how come the men we were chasing didn't?"

"That's exactly what I was about to ask you." Fraser smiled jovially at Frank. "They couldn't have run that close to the house. I wonder if they existed at all.''

Again, Joe was out of his chair. "You still don't believe us?"

"I think you boys are a bit—upset." Fraser held open his arms as if to say that wasn't a crime. "You're young and excited about the accident on the set. But this isn't a detective story. Leave the investigating to the pros."

Frank and Joe exchanged glances. For a moment Joe felt like revealing his true identity. But Frank's look kept him silent.

"This is a very wealthy town," Fraser went on. "Always open and ready for crime. But all in all, we've got the situation well in hand." He grinned. "Have you boys heard the history of the Newbridge jewels?"

Neither Frank nor Joe had.

"About a hundred years ago," Fraser told them, "ten of the wealthiest families in America decided to build luxurious oceanfront mansions along the cliffs of Newbridge. These homes would be their summer retreats.

"William Wedmont the third, by far the wealthiest of the group, came up with the idea for the Newbridge jewels," Fraser explained. "Each family, he suggested, would display their most precious gems in sealed showcases in the main parlor of each house. The original gems remain in these cases to this day."

Frank's eyes lit up. "Each collection must be worth millions," he said.

Fraser nodded. "So you see, because of the jewels, we always have men posted out there. It would be impossible for anyone to get by us at the Garfield mansion. There's extra private security there now, too, because of the filming."

"But they had to have found a way inside," Joe said. "It's the only place they could have gone."

Fraser chuckled and shook his head. "Impossible. Our alarm system is impenetrable."

"Tell me, Chief." Frank leaned forward in his chair. "Do you happen to know why the producers rented the Garfield mansion rather than any of the others?"

"Frankly, that surprised me," Fraser said. "I'd have thought they would shoot at the Wedmont place. It's more luxurious and was available earlier. The family will be away until the twenty-fifth." He shrugged. "Instead they held off shooting until the Garfields left."

The chief rang a buzzer on his desk. A moment later a police officer entered the office.

"I'm releasing these boys with just a warning," Fraser told the cop. He turned and glared at the Hardys. "That is, if they promise to keep out of trouble."

"Sometimes," Joe whispered to Frank, "that's a tough promise to keep."

The chief had the officer return Frank and Joe

to their van on Mansion Row. Not surprisingly, the Jaguar was now gone.

Why hadn't they suggested checking it out before they were taken in? Frank chided himself.

"Where to now?" Joe asked when the cop left.

Frank pulled the van into a U-turn. "Back to the airport," he said. "There must be evidence of sabotage in that helicopter. Why do you think we ran into those guys?"

"Sure," Joe agreed. "They must have been after the evidence, too."

Frank raced the van ahead. "I just hope we get back to the hangar before they destroy everything."

The hangar door was still locked when they arrived. No cars were parked out back. In fact, the entire area seemed deserted. Joe thought that was a good sign, but Frank wasn't so sure.

Hoping the window hadn't been locked, they ran around to the side. Frank went first, lifting the glass and climbing inside. Joe followed.

The lights were still out as they crept slowly across the floor to the chopper.

Suddenly Frank froze. He grabbed Joe's arm.

"I hear something," he whispered, listening intently. "Ticking!"

"Hit the deck!" Joe yelled, pulling Frank down with him.

But before they were down, the force of an

exploding bomb blasted them backward, knocking them hard against the wall.

Frank and Joe tumbled to the floor and rolled behind a Dumpster as the chopper burst into pieces, showering flames and burning shrapnel over the whole hangar.

Chapter

9

"OUT! QUICK, BEFORE everything blows!" Joe yelled, pulling Frank to his feet.

The hangar was filled with smoke and flaming debris. Sirens moaned in the distance, growing louder by the second. "We've got to find the door," Joe said, groping through the smoke.

"Here," Frank said.

He heaved against the hangar door, then he and Joe stumbled out, gasping in the fresh air. Frank blinked, his vision blurred from the smoke. There seemed to be a blue wall in front of him. Then he realized it was a line of men in blue uniforms—police officers, with guns in hand pointed at the Hardys. Two cops pushed them to the ground and handcuffed them with their arms behind their backs. Archie Fraser knelt to look at them.

"Hey, what gives, Chief?" Joe cried.

Fraser gave them a grim look. "Take them to headquarters," he ordered, "and get Sy Osserman on the phone. I think we've found his saboteurs."

"You've got it wrong, Chief," Frank said. "We came back here looking for evidence of sabotage. We figured we'd find it in the chopper. That's why the real saboteurs blew it up."

"Maybe," Fraser said. "But here's another scenario. Two brash stuntmen see their boss injured and want a police investigation. First they tell us about three thugs who disappeared into the Garfield mansion. When that doesn't work, they blow up the stunt helicopter to turn attention back on the case."

He smiled bitterly. "Well, you got *my* attention." He turned to his men. "Take them away."

Frank and Joe spent the next hour in the Newbridge jail. The cell was old and small, with one window high above their heads. Frank sat on the bed while Joe paced back and forth.

"They didn't properly arrest us," Joe complained. "They didn't even read us our rights."

"That's because we're not under arrest," Frank explained. "We're merely being held for questioning."

"Well, I just wish they'd get on with it then," Joe growled.

Finally an officer unlocked the iron gate and escorted them into Chief Fraser's office.

Sy Osserman, wearing a white suit, turned to greet them as they entered.

"I see you boys have gotten yourselves in hot water," he said, shaking his head in disapproval.

The chief's brow furrowed. "Mr. Osserman, destroying a helicopter is not hot water; it's a serious crime."

"We didn't destroy anything," Joe protested. "We explained what happened."

"Did word come through on that license plate?" Frank asked.

"Yes," Fraser said. "Oddly enough, no such number was ever issued in this state."

"But that can't be," Joe insisted. "I know I got the number right."

Sy Osserman sighed. He raised his hand and smiled. "Look, Chief, this is getting us nowhere. The producers have insurance that will cover the cost of the helicopter."

"That doesn't solve the criminal matter," Fraser said.

"I'll vouch for Frank and Joe," Osserman said, leaning across the chief's desk. "Besides they're two of my main stuntmen. I need them."

"Well . . ." Fraser considered.

Frank and Joe smiled at the chief. They knew that the film was important to Archie Fraser and the town of Newbridge.

"So far we've got nothing but circumstantial evidence tying them to the crime," Fraser said, nodding at the director. "So if you're willing to accept responsibility for them—"

"I'll keep a close eye on them at all times," Osserman assured him. "I promise."

The director turned to glare at the Hardys. "Boys, stop annoying the police chief. He doesn't have time for your antics. He's got enough on his hands just guarding the Newbridge jewels."

Frank raised an eyebrow. So Sy Osserman knows about the jewels, he thought. Maybe there was more going on than a simple case of sabotage.

Archie Fraser stood. "All right. I'm letting you fellows go. But if there's any more trouble, we'll be meeting again."

The chief escorted Osserman, Frank and Joe out to the director's waiting limousine. As the chauffeur pulled away, the director pushed a button to raise the soundproof glass.

He looked angrily at the Hardys. "I don't have time for these visits to the police station. What did you find out?"

Frank told him about their two visits to the airport. The news didn't please the director.

"So, all in all, you've got zilch," he said. "No evidence, no suspects—nothing but trouble."

The next day morale on the set was at an all-time low. People eyed one another suspiciously and all work went slowly. The main topics of conversation were the captain's accident and the possibility of sabotage.

When Frank and Joe entered the stuntmen's building they were surprised to see Sy Osserman and Ed Kemble in the lounge. Osserman raised his voice. "All stuntmen pull up chairs. I'm calling a meeting."

He looked around at the crew. "Because of yesterday's unfortunate accident, we need a new stunt chief. Therefore, I'm appointing Ed Kemble as the new stunt director."

Murmurs rippled through the audience. The dozen stunters seemed stunned, and clearly not everyone was pleased with the selection. Gil Driscoll seemed especially put off. His face turned red as he compressed his lips. "Politics," he griped. "I'm the best stuntman around, and they give the job to an actor."

But only Janet Wynn rose with an objection.

"Ed Kemble may be a star," she said. "But he doesn't have any experience running stunts."

Ed flashed her his famous smile.

"Janet's right," he said, stepping forward. "I've never been a stunt director. But I was a stuntman before I became an actor. I'm still in the union, and I've seen some of the greatest stunts in movie history. I can handle the job."

"I appreciate how Ed volunteered to take on this huge responsibility." Osserman slapped the actor on the back. "He's got some great ideas."

"Thanks, Sy," Ed said modestly, his eyes dropping down for just a moment.

He looked back at the team. "Now, our first task will be arranging for two major nighttime stunts. We have a high jump off the side of a building. And we have the flaming car flying over the side of the cliff."

"That's two more accidents waiting to happen," Gil growled.

Ed smiled at him. "I hope not, because I'm going to do the leap from the building."

He nodded at Janet. "The script calls for you, portraying Kitt Macklin, to join me. However, if you feel you need some time off—"

Janet shook her head. "No, I'll jump," she said. "It's my job. I can handle it."

"That's the spirit." Ed proudly raised a clenched fist. "Now we need someone to drive the burning car by the cliff."

Slowly his eyes scanned the team.

"Keep your fingers crossed," Joe whispered to his brother.

"Frank," Ed Kemble decided. "You look the most like Burke, and the camera may move in close."

Frank swallowed hard. He turned to look at Joe and shrugged. "See?" Joe scolded him. "You didn't have your fingers crossed."

After the meeting, the team got busy preparing for the evening's stunts. Frank and Joe joined the mechanics, watching closely as they tuned the shiny blue Maserati that would go off the cliff hours later. Frank took the car out for a practice spin, getting a feel for it.

Around noon, they broke for lunch. Frank and Joe headed for the food tent and found themselves in a cafeteria line with trays. "Just like school," Frank said. "I just hope the food is better."

Joe looked over the selection and shook his head. "Not likely," he said.

Frank and Joe spotted Janet, looking unhappy, seated at a small table.

"Maybe she'd cheer up if we brought her into the picture," Frank suggested.

Joe creased a brow. "What do you mean?"

"We know that she's not our saboteur," Frank said. "No way would she injure her own father."

"And if she was the bad guy," Joe added, "no way would she go to the police."

"What's more," Joe said, "we can use an ally."

Janet managed to smile as they approached her.

"How's your dad?" Joe asked, standing across from her with his tray.

"About the same, but the doctor says he will pull out of it. Do you want to sit down, Frank and Joe?"

"The Frank and Joe is right, but not the Harris," Frank said, pulling out his chair. "Our last name is Hardy."

Speaking in whispers, Frank and Joe told her of their undercover investigation and of their adventures at the airport.

Janet banged the table with her fist. Joe's vegetable soup slopped all over his tray.

"You see," she said excitedly. "That proves these accidents weren't my father's fault."

She stood and waited for Frank and Joe to join her. Joe picked up his sandwich and then Janet whisked them out the side door. "I've got something to show you."

She led them to the captain's trailer, dug out her key, and went in. She flicked on the lights then knelt to open a bottom dresser drawer.

"My father knows the stunts are being sabotaged," she explained. "So I began to wonder if maybe he was hurt because of what he knew. Maybe he'd gathered some evidence." She pulled a memo pad out from under a pile of sweaters. "This is what I found. The handwriting is my father's."

Frank and Joe read from the pad.

Stunt Materials Missing:

4 Twenty-Foot Wound Ropes
2 Pulleys
8 Flashlights
2 Sets of Walkie-Talkies
1 Wrench
1 Pair of Wire Clippers

"Why would anyone need all that stuff?" Joe wondered out loud.

"I don't know," Frank said. "The captain must have been close to finding out. If only we had seen that missing film."

"Yeah, the saboteur really fouled up and got caught by the camera. But he still managed to clear his tracks."

"Maybe *all* the tracks weren't covered," Frank said. "Maybe we just need a gimmick to flush him out."

"A gimmick." Janet rose to her feet. She took the pad from Joe and placed it back under the sweaters.

"Come on," she said, looking at her watch. "I've got to go practice my stunt. But I think I have the perfect idea." She led them back outside and locked the door. "Meet me at seven at my trailer. I'm going to bait and hook our fish."

"Janet." Frank grabbed her arm. "What have you got in mind?"

"You'll see."

"Don't play games," Joe warned her. "If you make the wrong move, you could get killed."

"My plan is perfect," she said, running off.

At seven Frank and Joe left the stunt building and headed for Janet's trailer.

"I wonder what she has in mind?" Joe said.

"I guess we're about to find out." Frank suddenly stopped and pointed across the lot. "There she is. Hey, Janet!"

But Janet didn't seem to hear. She kept walking toward her trailer. Frank and Joe followed the back of her black satin jacket, the logo for *The Lost Princess* glittering as she walked.

"Hey, Janet!" Joe shouted.

The girl glanced over her shoulder. When she spotted Frank and Joe approaching, she abruptly took off—away from them.

"Janet, stop!" Joe shouted.

But she didn't stop; she cut her way around props and crew members.

"Something's wrong," Frank said.

They chased her along a path, lost sight of her for a moment, then caught another glimpse of her jacket. Janet had a good lead, but Frank and Joe were faster. By the time she reached her trailer, she was just a few feet ahead.

She held the key in her hand, thrusting it up to unlock the door before they caught up to her.

Just as the key slipped in, Joe grabbed her by the shoulder. With a cry of fear, she spun around to face them.

Only it wasn't Janet.

It was Kitt Macklin!

Chapter
10

A STRAINED AND SICK expression came over Kitt Macklin's face.

"So, what have we here?" Joe asked, grinning at the actress.

"I—I, ah . . ." Kitt swallowed hard. She turned to Joe and flashed her movie star smile. "It's really all quite simple—and highly amusing, actually."

"So tell," Joe said. "We need a laugh."

"You know Burke's been flirting with Janet," Kitt whispered confidentially. "Well, I suspect a little romance has been going on behind my back. Burke denies the whole thing, but—"

"Why are you here?" Frank interrupted.

"But I don't believe him," Kitt went on, ignoring Frank's question. "I thought I'd check to see if he's sent her any more flowers."

"That still doesn't explain how you got Janet's jacket and keys."

"Janet was working, and her jacket was on a chair with the keys in its pocket." Kitt gave them a big grin. "So I thought I'd 'borrow' it for a while to check out her trailer."

Joe and Frank exchanged glances.

"You'll have to do better than that," Joe said. "The jacket story might have washed if you weren't also wearing similar jeans and the same color T-shirt and had your hair in a ponytail, the way Janet's been wearing hers."

"It was a good disguise for going into her trailer," Kitt told them.

"You went to all that trouble just looking for flowers?" Frank said. "Come on."

"So you think I'm lying?" Kitt raised her chin. She stepped off the stairs, but Joe grabbed her arm before she could walk away.

"Let go of me," she protested.

"Sure." Joe released her arm. "But I wish you'd level with us."

Tears welling up in her eyes, Kitt slumped down on the trailer steps. "Okay. There's also this." She reached into the back pocket of her jeans and pulled out a small white envelope. Frank unfolded the letter inside.

" 'I know who has the missing film,' " he read. "Signed, 'Janet Wynn.' " Frank glared at Kitt. "Is that why you're here? *You* have the film?"

"No!"

Suddenly Kitt was up, pushing Frank back and rushing past him. But she hadn't run more than a few steps when a canister of film flew out from under her jacket.

Kitt reached for the canister as it fell to the ground, but Frank scooped up the film while Joe grabbed her. "Look what I found," Frank said.

But he didn't have long to enjoy his discovery. From behind Janet's trailer, Burke Quinn ran forward. The actor roared like a madman, his hands aimed for Frank's throat. Frank turned just as Quinn charged him, and he nearly had the wind knocked out of him.

The film can flew up in the air. But Joe caught it before it hit the ground.

"Hit him, Burke," Kitt shouted, furious.

Quinn and Frank struggled and rolled around on the ground. Finally Frank managed to pin Quinn beneath him, his legs imprisoning the actor's arms.

"What gives?" Frank shouted. "Why'd you attack me?"

"You guys can't manhandle my girlfriend," the actor shouted back.

"Burke, you were defending me?" Kitt asked. "How wonderful."

"Did you also help Kitt steal the stunt film?" Frank asked.

"She didn't steal it," Quinn said. "*I* did."

Frank and Joe stared at him.

"I did it as a little prank. I wanted a private

viewing of some of the rushes in my trailer, that's all. But I didn't sabotage any stunts."

"But why did you just steal the stunt scenes?" Frank asked.

"I wanted to see if the action scenes were going to be strong enough. This is an action movie, and if it's not exciting, it won't sell."

Frank let go of the actor and helped him to his feet. Quinn took an envelope from his pocket and handed it to Frank, who read it quickly.

"It's the same as the one Kitt received," he said.

"I would have put the film back," Quinn explained. "Only after what happened to the captain, I was afraid to admit what I'd done."

"When these notes arrived," Kitt said, "we decided to stash the film in Janet's trailer."

"We hadn't even looked at them yet," Quinn added.

"Where are the rest of the reels?" Joe asked.

Kitt unzipped her jacket, slowly pulling out five more canisters. Grudgingly, she handed them over to Joe.

"What a relief," Joe said. "For a moment I thought you'd suddenly put on weight."

Kitt made a face. "What are you going to do now?"

"You're not going to turn us in, are you?" Burke Quinn sounded nervous.

"There's only one thing to do," Frank decided.

"Let's go view the reels and see if we can spot our saboteur."

Cal was in the projection booth when they arrived to view the missing reels. They took their seats while Cal threaded reel 242—Janet's motorcycle stunt scene—through the projector.

"Now we'll see if the captain's hunch was right," Frank said.

Before Janet's ride, the cameraman had taken a series of shots, first filming a wide-angle panoramic view of the set. Next the camera closed in on the road and fence. At last the scene settled in on Janet's motorcycle, following her down the road and into the fence. Joe winced as he once again watched her hit the wall and go up in flames.

"See anything suspicious?" Frank asked.

Kitt Macklin and Burke Quinn shook their heads.

"It all went by too fast," Joe said.

They watched the scene again, then a third time.

"Hold it," Frank said. "I think I see something. Cal? Can you slow this down?"

"Sure. I'll roll it one frame at a time." Cal fiddled with the projector. Then the scene appeared on the screen as still shots from a slide show.

"Right there!" Frank shouted.

In the corner of the picture, a man was standing by the fence, a gallon container in his hand.

Quickly he doused the fence with a clear liquid. Then for half a second—in the space of just three frames—the man turned toward the camera.

Joe's eyes opened wide. "It's Gil Driscoll."

"Stuntmen," Burke Quinn growled, putting his arm around Kitt. "You can't trust any of them."

Frank sat very still. "I was just thinking that Janet probably sent those notes, but she couldn't possibly have seen the film."

"Of course not," Joe agreed. "Sending those notes to Burke and Kitt was just a trick to expose the saboteur."

"But if she sent notes to Burke and Kitt, she sent notes to other people on the set as well."

"You don't think—" Joe slapped his forehead.

"Exactly," Frank said. "If Gil Driscoll got a letter, too, then Janet is in danger."

Joe looked at his watch. "And her next stunt begins in just a few minutes."

The entire crew seemed to be on hand to witness the film's most dangerous stunt: Janet and Ed free-falling from the top of the Garfield mansion.

When Frank and Joe reached the set, Janet and Ed were already up on the roof of the building, which was well lit. In fact, the whole area was lit up like day. On the ground, directly beneath them, two large air bags were being set up to break their falls.

"There's Gil!" Joe exclaimed.

The stuntman was helping to move Janet's air-bag into place. Slowly, with his back turned to the crowd, he reached inside his cowboy boot.

"A knife," Frank shouted. "He's got a knife!"

But the crowd was too loud and too excited to make sense of the warning. Frank and Joe pushed forward, struggling through the knot of people.

Everyone was looking up at Janet and Ed as Frank and Joe saw Gil Driscoll slash Janet's air bag. Slowly the air bag began to deflate.

"Stop the stunt!" Frank shouted, still pushing through the crowd. "Stop it!"

His shouts alerted the saboteur. Driscoll turned and spotted Frank and Joe battling their way toward him. They'd reached a temporary barricade set up to keep everyone at a safe distance.

"Hey!" a security man shouted as Joe hopped the wooden horses.

Driscoll took off. Joe ran after him, but the saboteur ducked around the side of the building. And when Joe turned the corner, Driscoll was gone—vanished into the darkness.

"A minute to action!" Sy Osserman called through his megaphone.

"Hold it! Don't jump!" Frank called up to the rooftop, as he scaled the wooden barricade.

But the crowd noise was too loud for the stunters above to hear. Before Frank could call out again, he was tackled by two security guards.

"Don't jump!" Frank continued to shout as the guards were dragging him off. "Look," he said to the security men. "You've got to stop the stunt. It's been sabotaged!"

The guards continued to drag him along.

Frank twisted in their grasp, kicking one guard behind the knee. As the man's legs buckled under him, Frank pushed him in front of his partner and ran for the building.

Joe was ahead of him, dodging the guards, who were coming for him like running backs.

Together, the Hardys entered the building and plunged up the tall, steep back stairs.

"Thirty seconds," Sy Osserman called.

Frank and Joe pulled themselves along the railing, taking the stairs three at a time. They heard the security men pounding along behind them. "We can't think of them now," Frank gasped, pushing Joe ahead. Joe felt his heart pounding. Never had he run up stairs so fast before.

They reached the trapdoor to the roof and Joe smashed his shoulder against it, Frank right on his heels. The fresh air revitalized them, and the sight of Janet, poised, ready to jump, pumped up their adrenaline, which made them scramble even faster.

"Action!" Sy Osserman bellowed.

"Janet, don't jump!" they screamed.

Joe dove forward, his arms straining to grab

hold of Janet's ankles. His chest hit the roof edge, and he teetered.

But Joe's straining hands came up inches short. Janet floated in the air just beyond his grasp.

Then she dropped like a stone, and fell to the ground below.

Chapter

11

"JANET!" JOE SCREAMED.

The crowd stared silently from below, while the camera rolled, capturing Janet's fall to certain death.

Down she dropped, seeming to pick up speed as she passed the top floor, then the third, the second . . .

Suddenly Ed Kemble, his arms and legs fluttering in the wind as if he were trying to fly, reached over and grabbed Janet!

Joe broke into a broad smile. This was his old screen hero Ed Kemble, coming to life before his eyes. He was taking a big risk, but by pulling Janet close to him, he was diverting her from her own air bag and over to his.

Arm in arm they descended the last two stories, to land hard, smack in the center of Ed's fully inflated air bag. Their bodies bounced up once, as if they'd hit a trampoline, then softly fell back to rest.

Instantly the crowd gathered around them. Janet gave Ed a hug and a kiss on the cheek. Ed smiled and waved at the crew. He was pleased to be cast as a hero again.

At the director's orders, the security men had brought Frank and Joe to his trailer. Osserman was now pacing back and forth before them, while the Hardys sat together on the couch, explaining the situation.

"You're saying Gil Driscoll sabotaged all the stunts?" Sy Osserman asked. "I can't believe it."

"Check out the air bag," Joe said. "It's slashed with a knife—and we saw him do it."

"We've got hard evidence against Driscoll, too," Frank added, handing the director the important canister of film. "We've recovered the missing rushes—"

Osserman's eyes lit up. "How?"

"That's not important," Frank cut in, protecting Kitt and Quinn. "What is important is that during the filming of Janet's motorcycle stunt, the camera caught Gil Driscoll sabotaging the fence."

"Are you certain it's Gil?" Osserman asked.

"He's only on film a few seconds," Joe explained. "But when you run the scene in slow motion, frame by frame, there's no doubt at all."

The director slapped his forehead. "I just can't believe it! Gil's one of the best stuntmen in the country. He earns top dollar for his craft. Why would he toss his entire career away?"

"Good question," Frank said.

"Maybe we should consider catching him to find out." Joe jumped to his feet. "He can't be far away yet. And if we call Chief Fraser to set up roadblocks—"

"No more police involvement!" Sy Osserman howled. "Once the cops nail him, they'll release the story to the press."

"Does that matter?" Frank asked. "He attempted murder. This is very serious."

"If the press finds out about this," Osserman asserted, shaking his head, "then, babe, believe me, we won't be able to shoot another scene. The set will be swamped with reporters."

"We'll give you just a couple of hours to figure out what to say to the press. Then you call the police. In the meantime, we'll try to catch him ourselves. Come on, Frank."

Sy Osserman held up his hands like a policeman halting traffic. "Not just yet, Joe."

"What do you mean, 'not just yet'?" Joe's eyes sparkled with anger. "You're not going to let him get away, are you?"

"Of course not!" The director slung his arm around Joe's shoulder. Joe brushed it aside. "But right now we've got Frank's stunt drive along the cliff to shoot."

"Another stunt?" Joe shuddered in disbelief.

"With all that's happened," Frank said, "I'd forgotten about it."

"Well, put it off then," Joe said angrily. "We've got a crook to catch."

"We can't put it off," the director asserted. "We're so far behind schedule, my job's already on the line. The crew has everything ready to go in fifteen minutes. Stunts cost too much to keep rescheduling. I've already lost the leap from the building. If I delay the night drive, who knows when the weather will be this clear again?"

Frank and Joe exchanged glances.

"All right," Frank said. "I'll do it."

"But, Frank—"

"What a guy!" The director beamed. "I knew I could count on you!"

"There's just one condition," Frank added.

"Anything you want." Osserman's voice was breathless with desperation. *"Anything."*

"Once this stunt's completed," Frank said, "you go straight to the police."

Sy Osserman shrugged. "It's a deal."

Quickly he led Frank and Joe out of the trailer to the waiting limousine.

"Let's hope I can convince Archie Fraser to keep all this quiet," Osserman said.

* * *

Ed Kemble and the crew were waiting to shoot the stunt out on the cliffs behind the Garfield mansion.

"We were worried you might not show up," Ed said, shaking Frank's hand when they emerged from the limo. "Wesley thought you might have gotten a case of the jitters. He thought he'd have to perform the stunt for you. 'Not Frank Harris,' I told him."

Frank smiled. "How could I back out on you after the way you saved Janet's life?"

"All in a night's work." Ed winked at Joe. "Anyhow, your brother deserves the credit. If I hadn't heard him shouting down at us as we flew off the building, I would have never suspected anything was wrong with the air bag."

Ed led Frank over to the blue Maserati. He opened the door and handed Frank his protective helmet. Next, Frank slipped a special flame-retardant suit over his own clothing.

He sat behind the wheel and thoroughly examined the car. Everything appeared to be in order, and with Gil Driscoll gone from the set, Frank felt relatively safe.

"All set?" Ed asked him.

"All set," Frank replied, turning to give the thumbs-up signal to Joe and Sy Osserman.

Frank sat behind the wheel. He adjusted the seat and the mirrors.

"This will be the shortest ride of your life," Ed told him. "Just a few hundred feet over to the cliff. In fact, for safety we've only filled your tank with enough special fuel to cover the distance.''

Ed smiled at Frank. ''Once the flames hit the car, we wouldn't want any extra fuel in that tank to blow you sky-high, would we?''

The path that Frank would follow was completely dark, but special fluorescent tape marked boulders along both sides of the strip so that Frank could see the way.

''We decided that absolute darkness would work best,'' Ed explained, ''so that when the explosion hits, the car will really illuminate.''

''I can hardly wait,'' Frank said dryly.

Ed chuckled. ''Don't worry. You know the Maserati is insulated with special protective shields. So while the outside of the car is burning, you'll be safe inside.''

''You make it sound easy,'' Frank said.

''It *is* easy,'' Ed assured him. ''The only tough part comes when the car is on fire. You won't be able to see through the flames, but all you have to do is drive straight ahead. That way you won't slide over the cliff.''

Frank gawked. ''What do you mean, slide over the cliff?''

''Once the explosion hits, just count to five and hit the brakes,'' Ed explained. ''That will give you plenty of room to stop.''

Frank looked skeptical. ''Once I do, how do I get out of the burning car?''

''Push open the driver's door and bail out,'' Ed

instructed. "The crew will move in to push the Maserati over the side of the cliff. That way we'll get a closeup of it smashing against the rocks below."

"Just make sure I'm out of the car before you push it over," Frank said.

Ed grinned. "I'll try to remember."

With Gil Driscoll gone from the set, Frank thought, this might just turn out like the piece of cake Ed Kemble made it sound.

Now he rolled up the window and revved the engine. Then he looked straight ahead at the path. Fifty feet in front of him an electronic device was rigged to set the car on fire as Frank passed. A hundred feet beyond that was the edge of the cliff. Frank could barely see where the sky met the ground in the darkness.

"Action!" Sy Osserman shouted through his megaphone.

Frank raced the car forward. He moved straight ahead, following the path that had been laid out for him.

But even in the darkness, some movement off to the side caught his eye. Gil Driscoll!

As Frank drove by, the man jumped up from behind a boulder. Frank could see Driscoll's twisted grin. He stood in the darkness, waving a fuel can above his head as Frank passed. The last drops of gasoline dripped from the can to the ground.

Instantly, Frank smelled the familiar odor.

Driscoll must have replaced the special fuel in the gas tank with regular gasoline. The moment the flames touched the Maserati, gasoline would send the blue sports car a mile high.

Desperately Frank tried to veer the car away from the path. But boulders on either side forced him back on course. He hit the brakes, but the car was moving too fast to stop him in time.

There was only one way out. *Jump!*

Frank grabbed the door handle. It didn't open. He reached over to try the passenger side. When he did, the handle came off in his hand. Frantically, he attempted to roll down the windows. They were sealed shut.

Sweat began to roll down his face. Within moments the flames would engulf the car and blow it to bits—with Frank trapped inside!

Chapter

12

DESPERATELY, FRANK RIPPED off his seat belt, pushing himself up till the top of his head touched the roof of the Maserati.

With one hand on the steering wheel to keep the car from swerving out of control, he braced himself against the car's roll bar. It had been specially designed to keep the roof from caving in if the stunt car overturned. Now it provided Frank with the support he needed to smash his way out.

With a wild cry, Frank smashed out with his leg in a karate kick against the driver's-side window.

The window shattered, sending glass in every direction. Ducking low, Frank dove forward, hurtling through the small open space the broken window had created.

Frank landed hard on his shoulder, then somersaulted head over heels as flames suddenly engulfed the Maserati. He scrambled away and lay flat on the ground as the car veered wildly out of control, spinning toward the cliff.

The explosion came just as the car flew over, lighting up the sky with a plume of bright orange flame. The fiery shell plunged toward the sea, smashing against the hard rocks and splitting into two burning pieces. A thick cloud of smoke rose above the cliffs as the car disappeared beneath the surface of the waves below.

"Frank!" Joe ran up to his brother, who lay flat on the ground. The rest of the crew swarmed behind him. They, too, had seen Frank's escape. "Are you hurt?"

"Only my professional pride," Frank said, allowing Joe to help him sit up. "I should have never let Sy Osserman talk me into performing a dangerous stunt with our friend still at large. That mistake nearly got me killed."

"Driscoll was responsible for this one, too?" Joe stared in disbelief. "But how? We saw him run off. I'd have thought he'd be miles away by now."

"It looks as if he believes killing us is a better plan than running," Frank said. "I spotted him behind a boulder as I passed. He was swinging an empty container of gasoline. Somehow, he was able to gas up the Maserati before the stunt."

Joe frowned and turned to Osserman. "It's

time we were going to the police. This is too dangerous to keep under wraps any longer."

"Absolutely," Frank agreed, scanning the crowd. "Let's get Janet and take her along with us. I want to be sure that she's safe."

"Janet!" Joe's eyes opened wide. "Oh, no!"

"Wasn't she with you watching the stunt?"

"I didn't see her," Joe said nervously. "She wasn't on the set. And with Gil Driscoll out of the way, we didn't think to keep an eye on her."

Frank held out his hand so that Joe could lift him to his feet.

"But Driscoll's *not* out of the way," Frank said. "What's more, he believes Janet has the evidence against him."

"Which means she's in great danger," Joe said grimly.

Sy Osserman and Ed Kemble were surveying the wreckage. Frank decided not to waste time with them. "Let's get out of here and find Janet," he said.

Osserman called after them, but Frank and Joe didn't even turn as they headed back to Janet's trailer. The Hardys dashed past the sets and equipment sheds to the crew's quarters. Janet's trailer was a good ten-minute run. As they approached, they heard a crash from inside, followed by the clumping of footsteps on the trailer's stairs. Janet let out a sudden cry, but her voice was quickly muffled.

"Come on!" Joe urgently whispered, taking off for the front of the trailer.

Two hooded men were dragging the struggling girl toward their car. A third hooded man sat impatiently behind the wheel. Even in the dark, Frank and Joe could tell it was the same black Jaguar they had chased from the airport.

The men carrying Janet looked like the two assailants who had pulled switchblades on the Hardys in the hangar. The shorter man had Janet by the legs, while his taller companion had a thick arm around her shoulders. His gloved hand covered her mouth.

"This time they won't get away!" Joe charged forward.

The hooded men quickly dumped Janet into the backseat. They attempted to climb in after her and drive off without a fight, but Joe was at the door before they could get away.

He hauled out the taller man by his belt, tossing him to the ground. Then he made a grab for Janet as the Jaguar suddenly moved forward.

Frank jumped on the hood, but the car swerved sharply, throwing him off. Joe ran up behind, and leaped for the back door. He missed by inches, when the car turned, and fell flat to the ground.

"Joe! Frank!" Janet screamed. "Help me!"

They scrambled to their feet to make another run for the Jaguar. Now the car had spun around and was heading back, straight for them.

"Jump!" Frank bellowed.

Joe leaped aside, tasting dust as the car plowed on past. The Jaguar barely missed him. Quickly it swerved around, trying to catch Frank.

Instead of jumping aside, Frank timed his leap and made it back onto the hood of the car. Through the windshield he glared at the hooded driver, wondering if it was Gil Driscoll. Hanging on as tightly as he could, he reached across for the passenger door as the car swerved wildly back and forth.

As his fingers touched the handle, the Jaguar suddenly screeched to a halt. Frank went flying, then landed hard on the ground, dazed and dusty. When he looked up, the taller goon was opening the back door and jumping inside. This time, the Jaguar took off, leaving the Hardys behind.

"Are you okay?" Joe asked, running over to Frank, as his older brother once again lay in the dirt. "You've had a rough night of it."

"Not as rough as Janet's had," Frank said.

Her trailer door had been left open. Frank and Joe leapt up the steps and had a look inside. The place looked like a tornado had struck. The furniture was overturned. Janet's clothing was scattered over the floor. Books and papers were ripped and thrown about. Even the mattress was torn.

"I'll bet they were very upset when they didn't find the film," Frank said.

Joe nodded. "Well, they couldn't find it, because Janet doesn't have it. She doesn't even know where it is."

"Yeah," Frank replied. "But we do. Sy Osserman has it, and soon he's going to turn it over to the police."

"Not before we get Janet back," Joe insisted. "We may need it to negotiate with them."

Frank nodded. "Let's get back to our hotel room. Once Gil is convinced that Janet doesn't know where the film is, he'll think we have it."

"And you're willing to set up an exchange?" Joe asked.

"If Gil Driscoll is."

"We've got nothing to give him," Joe reminded him.

"Well, what Driscoll doesn't know *can* hurt him," Frank said. "If we show up with one blank roll of film, maybe that'll buy us enough time to save Janet."

For the next hour Joe paced the motel room. Frank sat grimly on the bed, glancing every few minutes at the silent telephone.

"I hope they're not hurting her," Joe said.

"Janet's strong," Frank told him, even though he'd been worrying about the same thing.

Finally the phone rang.

Frank composed himself. He let it ring three times before he picked it up. Let Gil Driscoll believe Frank was as cold and as calculating as

Driscoll himself was, he thought. That might improve his bargaining position.

"Have you called the police?" Driscoll asked the moment Frank lifted the receiver.

"Of course not."

"Good," the saboteur said. "Just remember, if you try to involve them, Janet will meet a very unpleasant end."

"I understand," Frank said.

"I knew you would." Driscoll sounded pleased. "We want the film."

"We want Janet."

"Well, then, I believe a trade can be arranged," the saboteur said. "Bring the film to the wine cellar of the Garfield mansion."

"The wine cellar?" Frank said in disbelief. "But we'll never get in there tonight. The cops have the place wired. Any movement around the house and they'll spot us."

"Not if you guys don't break the silent alarm," Driscoll explained. "Walk along the cliffs until you come parallel to the house. Then walk in a straight line—one behind the other, not side by side—until you reach the wine cellar door."

"All right," Frank agreed. "But still, the cops might see us."

"Let's hope for Janet's sake, they don't."

Abruptly, Driscoll hung up the phone.

Frank and Joe drove out to Mansion Row. They parked near the wooded area between the Garfield and Wedmont mansions, just as they had after the chase from the airport. Slowly, they made their way through the trees and out to the cliff.

A heavy fog had just rolled in from the ocean, muffling all sounds. As Frank followed Joe he could hardly see the rocks they clambered over. But they could hear the waves pounding below.

They kept low and moved slowly, watching for any policemen patrolling the area.

Finally they drew parallel to the rear of the Garfield mansion. On a balcony above, one guard, a shotgun on his lap, snored away on a reclining chair. A second officer sat across from him, reading a magazine by flashlight.

"From here on in we've got to be absolutely quiet," Frank whispered. "Be sure to follow my footsteps exactly."

"Okay," Joe agreed. "And once in the cellar, no sudden moves until we've got Janet safe."

Frank nodded and led the way as the Hardys inched closer to the wine cellar door. Halfway to their destination, Joe stepped on a twig, loudly snapping it in two.

They ducked down against the side of the house as a flashlight beam scanned the area. But after a moment, the officer on the porch seemed satisfied, and went back to his magazine.

Frank and Joe continued on. The entrance to the wine cellar was slightly ajar. Slowly, they pulled it open and stepped down the steps. Inside, the cellar was pitch black.

Suddenly lights flashed on. But still they saw no one.

"Janet?" Joe called. "Are you here?"

" 'Fraid not, fellas."

From behind the shadows of a huge wine barrel, Gil Driscoll stepped out. In one hand he held two sets of handcuffs.

"Put 'em on," he said, tossing the cuffs over to Frank and Joe. "Lock them tight."

Against their better judgment, Frank and Joe did what they were told.

They didn't have a choice.

In Gil Driscoll's other hand, aimed at their chests, was a .44 Magnum revolver!

Chapter

13

LOCKED IN HANDCUFFS, Frank and Joe were at Gil Driscoll's mercy. We'll have to take our time, Frank thought, and wait for an opening.

"Did you bring the film?" Driscoll asked.

"You said we'd make an exchange," Frank shot back. "If you want the film, release us—and Janet."

That made Driscoll laugh uproariously.

"When someone points a gun at you," he said, "that's not the time to bargain."

The saboteur thumped a fist on the wine barrel. Responding to the signal, two men walked out from the shadows—the Hardys' old enemies from the airport hangar.

Roughly, the henchmen shoved the Hardys up against a barrel and carefully frisked them.

The taller man reached deep into Frank's safari jacket pocket.

"Look what we have here," he said, coming away with the reel of film.

When the man handed the canister over to Driscoll, Frank was able to get a good look at his face for the first time. It was Wesley!

"So we meet again," Wesley said, his shaven head gleaming even in the dim light.

The shorter man's identity was the real surprise.

"Ty!" Frank exclaimed. The stuntman gave him a toothless grin. His injured arm seemed miraculously healed, no longer needing a sling.

"To think I felt sorry for you hurting your arm in a sabotaged stunt," Joe said.

Ty merely chuckled. "I act a little, too."

"It was a neat trick," Driscoll boasted. "If Ty claimed to have been hurt and went around in a sling, who would ever suspect him?"

"It would also free up his time to help sabotage the other stunts," Frank reasoned.

Driscoll grinned at him. "You Harris brothers catch on pretty quick. A little too quick, I think."

He moved up close to peer in their faces.

"Who are you really?"

Frank and Joe remained silent.

"Okay." Driscoll shrugged. "We'll find out, of course, in due time. We have our ways."

That started Wesley laughing.

Slowly, Driscoll unwound the film and held it

up to the light. He studied the first frame carefully, and then the second. Angrily, he rolled out the entire reel to the floor.

"Blank!" he snarled. "That's a bad move, Harris!"

The back of his hand shot out across Frank's face. The slap hurt, but Frank stood still, his face expressionless.

"Where is the film?" Driscoll demanded.

"We'd have to be pretty dumb to walk in here and just hand it over to you," Joe said. "We want some assurance that Janet is okay."

Driscoll puckered his lips, considering things.

"Okay." He turned to Wesley and Ty. "Bring out the girl."

The crooks went and returned from a back room with Janet. Her hands were tied behind her back, and she was gagged. But at least she seemed okay, Joe thought. There were no signs that she'd been roughed up.

"Now," Driscoll said. "Where's the film?"

"Release Janet, and we'll send her to get it," Frank suggested. "We'll remain here as your hostages."

Again, Driscoll laughed. "If I let Janet go, she'll run straight to the police." The saboteur shook his head. "No, that won't do. Now that the three of you are aware of our little hideout, and know how to beat the alarm system, I can't let any of you leave."

"Then you won't get the film back," Joe told him.

"I was afraid of that," Driscoll said. "But I have other plans for you."

Frank shook his head, disgusted. "No matter what your plans, there's no way you'll get away with this. Why'd you sabotage the stunts, Gil? You had everything going for you—a great career, a reputation as one of the top stuntmen in Hollywood . . ."

Driscoll smiled. He moved close to the Hardys. Then he poked the barrel of the Magnum against Joe's chest, laughing as he cocked the gun. Joe didn't breathe.

"That was a pretty neat trick with the license plate," Frank said to Gil, trying to divert his attention. "How'd you get that fake plate, anyhow?"

It worked. Gil lowered the gun and turned to Frank.

"They were courtesy of the film's prop shop," Driscoll explained. "After all, it wouldn't be smart to use stolen plates on our stolen car, would it?"

"Why are you trying to destroy the film?" Frank asked.

"Why?" Driscoll smiled, as though he were agreeing that it was a good question. "Because I'm not one of the top stuntmen in Hollywood. I'm the greatest! Perhaps the greatest of all time. And with all my ability, am I given the authority to head the second unit? No! Am I allowed to direct the ingenious new stunts that I've conceived? No way! Instead, that washed-up old fool, Captain Ray Wynn, gets the job."

Janet shouted at him, but it came out as a muffled cry from beneath the handkerchief in her mouth.

Driscoll turned to face her. "Look, honey, your father is a fool, long past his prime. He couldn't fill my shoes if he were twenty years younger. Yet he gets the job of stunt director."

The saboteur held up his forefinger and shook it to make his point. All the while he smiled and nodded his head. Frank realized they were dealing with a madman.

"But I knew I'd get my revenge," Driscoll went on. "Not only on the captain, but also on that loudmouthed moron of a director, Osserman."

Driscoll held his fist high over his head and stared at his white knuckles. "Sabotage! Every stunt they could come up with, we found a way to ruin it. Every single one of them."

"And what was in it for you two?" Joe asked, turning to Wesley and Ty.

The two henchmen glanced at each other and laughed.

"Money," Wesley said. "More money than we can make in a lifetime of stunting."

"And where's this money coming from?" Frank inquired.

Ty grinned. "From the—"

"You'll find out soon enough," Driscoll said, cutting off Ty.

He turned to take in all three of his captives. "I must congratulate all of you. Your ability to escape death has been uncanny. However, that won't last much longer."

"You made too many mistakes already, Gil," Joe told him. "Give yourself up now, before you go too far."

Driscoll just shrugged. "Sure. I made the mistake of getting caught on film. Then, when I went to retrieve the reel from the screening room, I found it had already been stolen."

Driscoll turned to Janet, smiling. "But with your note, the situation seemed crystal clear. You'd have to be taken care of, just as we took care of your father when he got too suspicious."

Despite the fact that her arms were tied behind her back, Janet charged forward, with a high kick. Her foot caught Driscoll's shoulder, just missing his throat. He let out a howl, flying backward. Janet went to kick him again, but Wesley smashed her to the ground.

"Joe, don't!" Frank shouted.

But when he saw Janet being pushed around, Joe lost control. He lowered his shoulder and barreled into Wesley, sending him falling back against a crate of wine bottles.

"Hold it right there!" Ty ordered, holding a gun smack up against Joe's forehead.

Frank stepped forward, but Driscoll scooped up the Magnum. "Don't be stupid, Harris."

"I think we'd better follow orders," Frank whispered.

"Too bad," Ty said. "We owe you guys a couple of bruises."

"Yeah," Wesley agreed, rising to his feet. "Let's work them over."

"Not just yet," Driscoll told them. "I have a far more interesting proposition for our heroic young stuntmen."

Wesley and Ty grabbed Frank and Joe and pushed them down hard onto the cold stone floor. Driscoll sat before them. This time he kept the gun aimed on them.

"Take Janet back," Driscoll ordered his men, "and stay with her while I talk business with Frank and Joe."

Janet struggled, but the two stunters were too strong for her. Ty laughed as he tossed her over his shoulder and carried her back into the shadows.

"We have a wonderful situation on our hands," Driscoll told the Hardys once his henchmen had closed the door behind them. "All around us, the police patrol the grounds, completely unaware that we're here."

"How did you find the way to bypass the silent alarm?" Frank inquired.

Driscoll waved the question off. "None of your business. The important thing is, there are no police inside the mansion at night. The entire house is open to us. And do you know what they keep inside the Garfield mansion?''

Joe nodded. "The Newbridge jewels."

A smile spread across Driscoll's face. "Very good. You guys have been doing your home-work."

"Is that your plan?" Frank asked. "To steal the jewels?"

"Well," Driscoll considered, "they may not be as valuable as the Wedmont collection, but still they're worth millions." He thought about it some more. "And since we're here . . ." He shook his head. "But, no, I'm not going to steal them."

Frank and Joe gawked at him, then breathed sighs of relief. But their ease was short-lived.

"You'll steal them," Driscoll said.

Both Hardys glared at the saboteur, who threw back his head and laughed.

"That's right," he told them. "You two bright boys have figured out so much, you should have no trouble finding a way to pull off the crime of the century for me."

"We won't do it," Joe said.

Driscoll just shrugged and called, "Ty!" The stunt man returned, pushing Janet ahead of him, a gun to her head.

Glancing at his watch, Driscoll told them, "You have one minute to change your minds. If not, Ty will shoot Janet. Fifty-six seconds—"

"Don't do it!" Janet shouted.

Frank and Joe looked at each other as Driscoll counted down. "Ten—nine—eight—"

"All right," Frank gave in. "You win."

Driscoll seemed pleased. He whistled, and Wesley came out of the back with a big red sack over his shoulder. "Just like Santa Claus," Joe muttered bitterly.

Driscoll took a pair of walkie-talkies from the bag, handing one to Wesley and keeping the other for himself. Next, he removed a set of blueprints, spreading them before Frank and Joe.

"This is the floor plan of the Garfield mansion," he explained. "As you can see, the jewels are kept in a sealed glass case in the center of the main corridor. An electronic beam encircles the case. If anyone steps within five feet of the jewels, they break the beam and send a silent alarm to the cops. What's more, there's no way to dismantle it."

"So the jewel case is impenetrable," Frank said.

"No way," Driscoll said. "You haven't even tried to come up with a solution. Study the prints." He looked at his watch. "I'll give you ten minutes before we go up into the house."

"Ten!" Joe gasped. "That's impossible!"

"No, it's not!" Driscoll told him. "Our sack of goodies has everything you'll need." He opened it up and looked inside. "We've got rope, pulleys, flashlights, wrenches, and screwdrivers."

Those were the items, Frank realized, that the captain had found missing from the stunt building.

"Oh. That's a whole new ballgame," Joe said.

"It's no laughing matter." Driscoll's expression turned stone cold. "I'll be upstairs with you, in touch by walkie-talkie with Wesley. Make any mistakes, or false moves, and Janet gets iced."

"All right," Frank said, rising to his feet. "Let's get on with it."

Driscoll uncuffed them, his eyes wide. "Can you get to the jewels?"

"I have an idea." Frank frowned. "But I'll have to see the actual case to know for sure."

Driscoll motioned for the Hardys to climb up the ladder in the corner of the wine cellar and open the hatch that led directly into the mansion. Joe went first, carrying the sack. Frank followed with the blueprints, and Driscoll brought up the rear with the walkie-talkie and gun.

"Stick close and wait for my signal," Frank whispered to Joe as they moved up through the hatch.

They found themselves in a pantry off the kitchen. Frank looked at the blueprints. "Okay," he said. "Through this door."

As they crossed the kitchen into the hallway, Frank raised his arm for silence.

Footsteps were coming, light but fast across the wood floor. Frank, Joe, and Driscoll ducked back against the wall.

"They're coming closer," Frank whispered, his heart pounding.

Two German shepherds padded forward, sniffing. Then their black eyes caught sight of the intruders.

"Guard dogs!" Joe warned.

Snarling, with saliva dripping from their fangs, the dogs sprinted toward them, closing in for the kill!

Chapter

14

As the slavering dogs bounded for them, Gil Driscoll jumped back, pushing open the kitchen door. He and the Hardys piled inside. Desperate, Frank and Joe heaved against the door, keeping the barking, scratching dogs outside.

"You're sunk, Gil," Frank said. "Every cop within a mile of this place must have heard that yapping."

But Driscoll shook his head smugly. "All the cops are outside the mansion, and the walls are completely soundproof." He raised his revolver. "Let those hounds in. I'll take care of them."

Frank shook his head, still holding the door. "I wouldn't bet on the walls being *that* soundproof." He spotted a stool at the counter, grabbed it, and wedged it against the door. "Relax, Joe," he said. "That'll hold them."

"Great," Joe said. "Only now we're trapped."

Driscoll climbed onto the high counter, shaking his head in reproach. "I'm surprised at you, letting a pair of pups scare you off."

Joe placed his hands on his hips. "Yeah? Do you have any suggestions for dealing with this?"

"Other than shooting them," Frank added.

Driscoll sighed, almost bored. "Check the sack, Joe—see what you've got to work with."

Joe's eyebrows rose as he rummaged in the bag. At first, all he felt were the ropes and other tools. But at the bottom of the sack was something else.

"Steaks?" he said, astonished, pulling them from the sack.

"Laced with tranquilizers," Driscoll told him. "Toss the meat on the floor, tie a rope to the chair, and climb up here on the counter."

Frank and Joe did as they were told.

"It's a gag from a flick I worked on years ago, called *Beware the Beasts*," Driscoll said.

Joe nodded. It was an Ed Kemble film he'd seen with Iola. She'd kept her head on Joe's shoulder each time Ed had confronted the pack of savage dogs.

"Okay, Frank," Driscoll ordered. "Pull on the rope."

Frank jerked it back, releasing the chair. The door swung open, and the two shepherds rushed into the kitchen.

To Frank and Joe's dismay, the dogs ignored

the steaks, leaping for the high counter. One nearly caught Joe's leg. The dogs kept jumping until, tired, they merely held their ground, barking and growling. Frank, Joe, and Driscoll remained quiet and still on the counter.

At last the shepherds turned to the steaks. "They're well trained," Driscoll said admiringly. "Usually the pups go straight for the meat. These two held out."

The dogs ripped the steaks to pieces, gobbling the meat. Then they yawned and lay down to rest. Soon their eyes closed, and they were fast asleep on the kitchen floor.

"One obstacle out of the way," Driscoll said happily, climbing down from the counter. "Now there're just the silent alarms to avoid."

"Sure," Joe agreed sourly. "Nothing to it."

The path to the main corridor was now open. All that remained between the Hardys and the jewels was the eight-foot-high, cylinder-shaped glass case in the center of the room, with its supersensitive alarm system.

Still, Frank, Joe, and Driscoll went slowly down the hallway. Frank kept his finger on the blueprints as they crept along. Every step of the way, Driscoll reported their movements back to Wesley via walkie-talkie.

"Quit stalling," Driscoll ordered at last. "Let's get the jewels."

Slowly they entered the corridor. The room beyond was dark. Only the gleam of the gems in their case provided any light. Frank and Joe stood motionless, staring at the precious stones.

"Magnificent," Driscoll whispered. "And soon they'll all be ours."

Joe took a step forward for a closer look, but Frank held him back. "See those little green lights?" He pointed up to the top of the eight-foot case. "That's where the electronic beam shoots down from."

"No wonder the case is circular," Joe said. "The alarm covers all possible angles of entry."

"Right," Frank agreed. "And that means we can't reach the jewels from in here."

"So what does that mean?" Driscoll's face was hot with anger. "You figuring on getting the jewels from a store downtown?"

"No." Slowly Frank pointed to the second-floor balcony. "We'll get them from up there."

Driscoll led the Hardys up the stairs to the second floor. The main corridor had a cathedral ceiling, nearly forty feet high. The second-floor landing was a good twenty-five feet above the ground. Even the tall, circular glass case looked small from up there.

"Okay." Frank observed the scene. "There doesn't appear to be an alarm system covering the top of the case. That's the vulnerable spot."

"But how do you figure on reaching the case from up here?" Joe asked.

"My question exactly," Driscoll said.

"We'll run two ropes across, from one side of

the landing to the other,'' Frank explained. ''Then, we'll put pulleys on the ropes and glide over to the top of the case.''

Driscoll repeated Frank's idea to Wesley over the walkie-talkie.

''Joe,'' Frank instructed, ''go across to the opposite landing. I'll toss you the ropes. Tie your end tight around that center beam.''

Again, Driscoll repeated these instructions to Wesley. Then he took the ropes. ''Let a pro take care of the lassoing. I've done enough cowboy films to do it right—and we don't want any clumsy throwing setting off the alarms.''

In seconds he had a lariat made, and sent it spinning out to Joe. It crossed the twenty-foot space easily, as did his second toss.

''Now we attach the pulleys.'' Frank hooked them on and the mechanism was set. He wheeled the pulleys out over the jewel case on a practice run.

''Do you think it'll hold the weight of a man?'' Driscoll asked.

''*Two* men,'' Frank said. ''If we're going to open that case, both Joe and I will have to swing across.'' He looked hopefully at the saboteur. ''Unless, of course, you want to try it yourself.''

''Not this time,'' Driscoll told him.

''I think we're set,'' Frank told him. ''Now we need flashlights, a screwdriver, and two pairs of gloves.''

"Absolutely." Driscoll handed out all of the necessary items from the sack.

Frank pulled the gloves on. He tossed the sack over his back, stepped over the railing, and got a good hold on the pulley.

"Okay," he said. "Here goes."

Holding the pulley with both hands, Frank jumped off the railing and slid across the open corridor. Slowly he came to rest directly above the jewel case. The rope sagged under his weight, but it didn't break.

"Your turn, Joe," he called out.

Joe gave the thumbs-up signal. Like a sky diver, he jumped off the opposite railing and rolled his pulley across to Frank. The rope bounced him for a moment, and then was still.

Frank handed Joe his pair of gloves.

"This is the tricky part," he said. "Do you want to hold me while I unscrew the hinges on the top of the case, or should I hold you?"

"You hold me," Joe said. "I think better on my head."

Joe drew up close to Frank so that his brother could get a tight grip around his waist. Then he released himself from the pulley. Carefully, Joe flipped down to face the ground. The sight of the floor twenty feet below made him swallow hard. But after a moment he was set to work.

"Okay, Joe," Frank told him. "When I lower you down, lock your legs with mine, just as trapeze artists do."

"Easy does it, Joe," Driscoll cheered him on. "Easy."

Joe locked his legs in Frank's. Joe released one hand, and when he was sure that his legs would hold, he let go of the other, to dangle above the glass case.

"Here's the screwdriver," Frank said, handing it down. "I'm going to lower you down to the case. Remember, be careful not to break the invisible beam. Stay within the green lights. Once you've accomplished that, remove the screws on top of the case."

Joe kept his arms close to his shoulders as Frank lowered him within the circle of green lights. He felt his legs stiffen as he balanced himself carefully against the glass and inserted the screwdriver into the first bolt.

"One down, three to go," he whispered.

Within five minutes, the cover was loose.

"Okay, Joe." Frank's voice was tight. "Carefully lift it up and I'll put it in the sack. Remember, don't break the invisible beam."

Joe handed Frank the pane of glass.

The gems lay on a black velvet base. Their brilliant sparkle was nearly hypnotizing. Joe couldn't help but stare at them in admiration. At last he reached down, his gloved hand coming away with the first necklace.

"He's got it," Driscoll said excitedly into his walkie-talkie. "He's got it!"

One by one, Joe handed each gem up to Frank. Quickly Frank placed them in the sack.

"Just one more," Joe said, grabbing a last gold watch and handing it up over his shoulder. "Okay, now how do I get out of this?"

"I'll pull you up above the beam," Frank said. "Once you clear the green lights, swing up and grab hold of the rope."

Slowly Joe rose back over the top of the glass case. Then, spreading out his arms, he heaved forward and whirled around, his legs releasing from Frank's. His right arm missed the rope, but just before he began the long fall to the floor below, his left hand clamped on.

Frank led the way as they slid the pulley back safely to the landing.

Driscoll was waiting for them as they climbed back over the rail.

"Here are your jewels," Frank said, swinging the sack across. "Now we want Janet."

"Jewels?" Driscoll actually seemed surprised. "*You're* the ones who stole them."

Suddenly he shoved Joe. Frank caught him before he toppled over the balcony.

The crook ran around the landing.

"Come on," Frank cried. "We've been double-crossed!"

Dashing around the bend, they closed in on Driscoll. But as Frank reached out to grab him, the saboteur pushed open a door and disappeared. Frank tried the handle. But the door was locked.

"Hold it right there!"

Frank and Joe froze. Joe closed his eyes. He didn't even bother to look.

"Archie Fraser," he moaned, shaking his head.

The heavyset chief of police puffed up the stairs, followed by about half his force. "Caught you red-handed," he proclaimed.

"And this time you'll be going away for a long, long time!"

Chapter

15

ARCHIE FRASER LEANED back in his rickety chair, rolling his eyes up at the ceiling. "We searched both mansions, like you asked," the chief said. "The only crooks we found were you two!"

"They must have escaped before you got to them," Frank said. "After all, they made their way in without your men spotting them."

"That's a really wonderful tale!" Fraser exclaimed. "Too bad you didn't stay in the movie business instead of becoming jewel thieves."

Joe jumped up. "But it's all true!"

"And we can verify it," Frank said. "Just call Sy Osserman. He'll back us up."

"Oh, of course." Throughout the interview, Fraser had spoken in a mock-pleasant tone that indicated he found everything Frank and Joe said to be farfetched. Still, the chief dialed the director's number and told the Hardys' story. All Frank and Joe could do was watch as Archie Fraser grinned and nodded to Sy Osserman's responses.

"I have the Harris brothers right here in my office," Fraser said at last. "I'll put you on the speaker phone so that they can hear you." He pushed a button, then Frank and Joe heard the director breathe heavily through the speaker box.

"Mr. Osserman," the chief began. "Did you hire a Frank and Joe Hardy to work as undercover operatives on your set, under the aliases of Frank and Joe Harris?"

"I don't know any Frank and Joe Hardy," Osserman stated.

Joe shot up from his chair, but Frank placed a hand on his shoulder to hold him back.

"We hired Frank and Joe Harris as stunt apprentices," Osserman continued. "They had good union credentials."

"Credentials he forged for us," Joe shouted.

Fraser merely glared at him. "Thank you, Mr. Osserman. Now, these fellas also claim they provided you with filmed evidence of Gil Driscoll sabotaging a stunt. Do you have such a film?"

"Why, no." Osserman sounded perplexed.

"And Janet Wynn. They claim she's been kidnapped," the chief went on. "Have you seen the young lady in question?"

"Of course I have." Now the director sounded

astonished. "She performed a stunt this evening."

"It happened after the stunt," Joe roared.

"Has anyone reported her missing? Or did anyone report witnessing a struggle?"

"No, sir," Osserman assured the chief. "I must compliment you on bringing our troubles to an end. Now that you've caught these two, I'm sure we'll have no more problems on the set. But for the sake of the picture, can you please keep this matter out of the press till we finish shooting?"

Fraser agreed, hung up, then called in two of his officers. "Let these two make their phone calls," he said, "then lock them up."

The officers took Frank and Joe roughly by the arms.

"Too bad it's now Saturday morning, guys," Fraser told them with a nasty grin. "The judge won't be behind the bench until Monday."

Frank turned and stared at the chief. "You mean we can't make bail over the weekend?"

"Sorry." The chief didn't sound all that sad. "For the next forty-eight hours you'll reside in a Newbridge jail cell."

As the officers started marching them out, Frank held back a second, looking at the chief. "Okay, you've got us," he said. "There's just one thing I don't understand. We pulled this job perfectly. I'm sure we didn't trip the alarm. So how'd you know we were in the mansion?"

The chief grinned. "Oh, I have my ways."

"What ways? We really want to know." Frank smiled. "It's for the book about the heist we'll spend the next twenty years in prison writing."

Fraser raised an eyebrow. "The what?"

"Should we call you Archibald Fraser," Frank went on, "or just plain Archie?"

"A book, huh?" Fraser laughed. He leaned back in his chair and thought it over. Clearly, he liked the idea. "Well, to tell you the truth, the crime was perfect. I'd even say brilliant."

"Then how'd you catch us?"

"By an anonymous tip."

The officers allowed Frank and Joe to make their phone calls. Frank dialed the emergency number that Fenton Hardy had given them. But their father wasn't there. The best they could do was leave a message for him and hope that Fenton would find a way to get them out of jail.

After the call, Frank and Joe were fingerprinted and photographed—they'd already been searched at the mansion. Then they were taken back to their cell. "I'm beginning to get used to this place," Joe said, straight-faced. "Still, I wouldn't want to call it home."

He grinned at Frank, trying to cheer him up. But his brother glumly stared out the barred window. "Why do you suppose Driscoll's guys tipped off the cops?" Frank asked after a while.

"You've got me," Joe said.

Frank shook his head. "It doesn't make any sense. They could have had the jewels."

Joe sat across from Frank on his thin mattress. "That's not the only thing that doesn't make sense," he added. "When you handed Driscoll the sack, he didn't even look inside. Instead, he tried to push me over the balcony rail, and he made a run for it. Why was he running? He had us at gunpoint."

Frank slapped his knee. "He was running because he knew the police would arrive any second, and he had to make his escape."

"Then why not take the jewels?" Joe asked, confused.

"He left them behind so we'd be framed." Abruptly, Frank rose from his mattress and paced back and forth across the cell. "That means Driscoll wasn't really interested in the Garfield collection after all." Frank smiled at his realization. "What he was interested in was our method for stealing them!"

"That's why he relayed every move we made over the walkie-talkie," Joe said. "No doubt Wesley took careful notes. All of which leaves me with just one question: Why?"

"I've been wondering myself," Frank said. "If Driscoll and company wanted to learn our method, they could only have one scheme in mind."

"Another robbery," Joe reasoned.

"You got it!" Frank said.

"Okay," Joe agreed. "But where?"

Frank laughed, making Joe stare. Being thrown in a jail cell didn't usually put Frank in a good mood.

"Chief Archie Fraser gave us the answer himself," Frank said. "Remember when he told us about the Newbridge jewels, saying the most precious gems were displayed in the Wedmont mansion?"

"And that all the mansions had similar layouts," Joe said, "meaning they could rob the Wedmonts the exact same way we robbed the Garfields."

Frank dropped to his mattress and held his head in his hands. "I just realized something," he muttered. "The chief told us the Wedmonts wouldn't be back in Newbridge till the twenty-fifth."

"That's tomorrow, Sunday," Joe said. "Well, I think it is. It's one in the morning now, so it's Saturday the twenty-fourth."

Frank nodded. "Which means the theft must take place between now and the morning."

Joe jumped up. "We've got to warn Fraser."

"I don't think he's exactly ready to believe us," Frank said. "What makes it worse is that if Driscoll pulls the robbery off, *we* get the blame."

"But why?" Joe cried desperately. "We're locked in jail. How could we commit the crime?"

"Since the Wedmont mansion has been empty all month," Frank explained, "the police will believe that the house was robbed before the Garfield mansion. And since they've already caught us for one theft, naturally they'll believe we knocked off the Wedmont place as well."

Archie Fraser was willing to give Frank and Joe another interview. But when he heard their warning instead of the confession he expected, the chief's patience disappeared.

"Look here, Harris, or Hardy, or whoever you've decided to be," Fraser bellowed at Frank. "I don't want to hear any more fantastic stories. The Wedmont mansion is completely secure."

"That's what you said about the Garfield mansion," Joe pointed out.

Fraser grew defensive. "It *was* secure. We caught you red-handed, didn't we?"

"Only because Gil Driscoll's men turned us in," Joe said.

"Oh, that's right, Gil Driscoll, the criminal mastermind." Fraser pounded his desk. "Listen, you guys will have to do better than that."

He turned to the officer who had brought the Hardys out from the cell. "Take them back," Fraser ordered. "And I don't want to see these two out of their cells until they go before the judge on Monday morning."

"Believe me, Chief," Frank urged. "Just this night you've got to provide extra security for the

Wedmont estate.'' The officer grabbed Frank's arm. ''You've got to!''

Hours of monotony followed as Frank and Joe spent all of Saturday trapped in their cell. As the sun went down for the evening, their guard approached to inform them that they had visitors.

The Hardys looked at each other, astounded. They had no idea anyone in Newbridge knew of their arrest, except for Sy Osserman, and surely he wouldn't be coming to see them now.

''Maybe Dad sent us someone who can help,'' Joe said, hope rising in his eyes.

But when the outer door opened, Frank and Joe were surprised to see Burke Quinn and Kitt Macklin.

''I always wanted to meet actual jailbirds,'' Kitt said sweetly.

The stars sat across a table from Frank and Joe, while a guard watched from beside the door.

''How'd you hear about us?'' Frank asked in a whisper.

''Everyone on the set is talking about your arrest,'' Kitt said.

''We appreciate the way you got the missing film back to Sy Osserman without pinning any of the blame on us,'' Quinn said with a grin.

''So if there's anything we can do for you, let us know,'' Kitt offered.

''If only there were,'' Joe said.

"There might be something," Quinn told him.

Slowly he reached into his pants pocket, then coughed, raising his hand to cover his mouth. A quick twist showed Frank and Joe what he was holding. Burke had smuggled in a cherry tomato!

"These local cops were a little reluctant to search a big star like me," Quinn bragged.

"Listen, Burke," Frank began. "Don't be fool—"

"Okay, time's up," the guard growled, coming up behind them.

Quinn and Kitt stood. Then, as they turned to leave, the actor brought back his hand.

"No!" Frank shouted.

But it was too late. Quinn threw the cherry tomato down at the guard's feet.

Poof! A cloud of thick red smoke rose up. The officer coughed hard, stumbling blindly ahead.

"Frank! Joe! Run!" Quinn shouted.

Frank and Joe didn't move. Out from the smoke screen came the officer, gun in hand. He wavered blindly, his eyes watering.

But he obviously made out Burke Quinn's shape. His weapon came up, pointed directly at the actor's head!

Chapter

16

BURKE QUINN STARED terrified down the barrel of the guard's gun. Frantically, he waved his arms before his face and shook his head. The guard, still dazed from the smoke of the cherry tomato, drew back the trigger!

But the gun didn't fire. Leaping over the table, Frank dive-tackled the guard, grabbed his gun hand, and knocked the weapon to the ground.

The guard reeled back but slammed his fist into Frank's jaw. Dazed, Frank still kept the officer in a bear hug. Got to stop him from ringing the alarm for help, he thought.

He swung the guard around, then released him with a hard shove. The guard tottered back, crashing to the floor of the open holding cell. Before he could get to his feet, Joe raced over to the gate and slammed it shut.

In a fury, the guard banged ferociously on the bars.

"Relax," Joe told him. "You've got a cell all to yourself. I had to share mine."

Frank was in no mood for humor. He rubbed his sore jaw, then grabbed Burke Quinn by the arm. "This is some mess you've gotten us in," he barked at the star. "We've just broken the law. Now we're escaped prisoners, and you two are accomplices."

"We can sort all that out later," Joe told him. "Right now, let's get out of here."

"Right," Frank agreed. "We've got a robbery to stop."

He turned to Burke and Kitt. "No one suspects you've done anything wrong," Frank told them. "You two can walk right out the front door. Act natural, as if nothing's happened. Then get your car and bring it around to the back entrance. And be sure to keep the motor running."

Frank and Joe waited a few minutes until they saw Burke and Kitt through the window, driving a gray Mercedes convertible around the back.

"Now it's our turn," Frank said. "We'll play it casual, walking out as if we're perfectly free to leave. Maybe we'll get to the door with no interference."

"And what if we don't?" Joe asked.

Frank's face went grim. "Then we'll do what we have to do."

To reach the back door, they had to walk down

a long hallway, turn a corner and climb a staircase, then follow another hall to the exit. Fortunately, they didn't encounter any guards until they rounded the bend. One officer sat by the staircase, but he merely raised his eyes from his newspaper and nodded at the Hardys as they strolled past him onto the stairs.

When they reached the landing, the doorway was in sight. So were the two burly officers sitting on either side of the door.

"Great," Joe whispered.

Slowly the Hardys came up to the officers. The cops waited motionless, watching Frank and Joe.

"Visitor's pass, please," the guard on the left asked Joe.

Joe reached down as though to check his pockets. Then he suddenly grabbed the policeman by the arm and jerked him from his seat onto the floor.

The other guard jumped up, his hand going for his holster. But a karate blow from Frank numbed the cop's arm, and another sent the officer sprawling on the ground.

Frank and Joe dashed through the door, sprinting for the waiting Mercedes. The cops shouted after them as they vaulted into the convertible, squeezing in behind Quinn and Kitt.

"Take off!" Frank ordered.

Tires squealed as Quinn floored the gas and

sped away. In the distance they heard sirens wailing as the police began their pursuit.

"Turn some corners," Frank told Quinn. "Lose them!"

Quinn couldn't have been more pleased. Like a professional race driver, he sliced the Mercedes around sharp curves, darting up and down the narrow streets of Newbridge.

"All right." Frank placed an arm on Quinn's shoulder. "You can slow down now. We've lost them."

"Hey," Quinn complained, "I was having fun."

The Hardys had the actor take them around to Mansion Row.

"I'd lay low for twenty-four hours," Frank advised the two stars as he and Joe jumped out of the car. "By that time we should have this entire mess cleared up."

Quinn saluted them army style, and Kitt blew each of them a kiss as they drove off.

Once the Mercedes was gone, Frank and Joe hit the wooded trail between the Garfield and Wedmont mansions. From the edge of the trees, they could see the Wedmont house, silhouetted in the darkness.

"Looks like Chief Fraser didn't take our advice," Frank said. "I don't see an officer in sight."

Joe sighed. "Driscoll's luck is still running high."

Since the Wedmont mansion wasn't open to the film crew, the Hardys were able to approach the house without fear of running through a gauntlet of police.

"Our only problem will be getting into the mansion itself," Frank said.

But when they reached the front entrance, they were amazed to find the door slightly ajar!

"Your hunch was right, Frank," Joe told him. "Now we know for sure that Driscoll and his boys are inside."

Frank examined the doorway. An extra wire, which didn't seem to be part of the alarm system, was attached to the top of the door.

"They've enlarged the alarm circuit," Frank explained, tracing the wire. "That lets them open the door enough to squeeze inside without triggering the alarm."

"Then suck in your gut," Joe whispered. "We'll go in the same way."

As Archie Fraser had told them, the floor plans of the two mansions were similar. Even with the lights off, Frank and Joe had no trouble finding their way to the main corridor.

They paused at the kitchen door to look in— and found two German shepherds sprawled silently on the floor.

Joe pointed to some scraps of meat on the floor. "They used the steak trick again," he said in a low voice. "These dogs are out for the night."

They continued down the corridor, clinging to

the walls so they wouldn't be seen by Driscoll and his men.

"Look," Joe whispered as they slowly ascended the staircase. "There's Janet!"

The stunt girl sat on the stairs with her hands tied behind her back. Gil Driscoll was by her side, issuing instructions to Wesley and Ty.

Hanging from the ropes over the center of the jewel case, his two henchmen were duplicating the robbery Frank and Joe had perfected in the Garfield mansion.

"I'll grab Driscoll," Frank decided. "You stop Wesley and Ty from sliding back to the landing."

"Sure thing," Joe said, rubbing his palms in anticipation. "Let's go!"

Driscoll stared in utter disbelief as the Hardys charged up the stairs. He'd been sure Frank and Joe would be out of their hair. Now shock slowed his reaction. He went for the gun wedged in his belt, but by the time the Magnum was out, Frank had grabbed his wrist.

Driscoll smashed a fist into Frank's rib cage. The blow made Frank wince, but still he kept his grip on Driscoll's hand. Steadily, he pulled the saboteur over to the edge of the banister and slammed his hand down hard against the rail. The gun dropped to the floor below.

Still, Driscoll wasn't finished. His free arm reached around Frank's neck, pulling him into a headlock. Frank elbowed him hard in the stomach, yet he couldn't break free. He drew back his arm for another hard poke, when suddenly Gil Driscoll released Frank, cried out in pain, and went rolling down the stairs.

Looking up, Frank realized the source of Driscoll's discomfort. Janet Wynn stood before him with a wide smile on her face. She had reared back like a football kicker and booted Driscoll behind the knee. The saboteur moaned loudly, clasping his leg.

Meanwhile, Wesley and Ty placed the jewel heist on hold as they desperately tried to slide back on their pulleys to reach the landing.

Before they'd traveled ten feet, Joe cut them off. He grabbed the ends of the support ropes, shaking them up and down. The two stunters could do nothing more than hold on for dear life.

As a finishing touch, Joe twisted the ropes into a huge knot. The henchmen became so entangled that the pulleys wouldn't roll. Helplessly, they dangled in midair.

"Hang in there, guys," Joe called out.

He turned and untied Janet's wrists while Frank went down and picked up Driscoll's gun. The saboteur looked up to find Frank, Joe, and Janet all standing menacingly over him.

"Start talking," Frank commanded. "Who's the real brains of this operation?"

"What do you mean?" Driscoll blustered. "I'm running this show."

Even Joe and Janet stared incredulously at

Frank. "If he's not in charge, who is?" Janet asked.

"The very man who saved your life," Frank told her.

"Ed Kemble?" Joe was horrified that Frank was accusing his old hero. "How do you figure that?"

"There were too many little indicators that slowly added up," Frank explained. "First, Ed Kemble always seemed to be hanging around with the stuntmen. So he could easily have coordinated these guys' activities.

"Second, Gil seemed to protest a little too much when Ed was made stunt captain. That made me suspicious, since they had been such good friends."

"Third, there's the whole jewel heist setup. Gil kept referring to it as 'our' plan. This whole complex scheme needed information that would be tough for a bunch of stuntmen to get—but easy for a star. You'd just about have to live here to discover a way around the alarm system. If we asked Sy Osserman, I'd bet one of his stars convinced him to rent the Garfield mansion, specifically. And if we interviewed the Garfields, we'd find that Ed Kemble had been a guest sometime prior to the filming."

"It was last September, to be exact."

Frank and Joe whirled. Ed Kemble stepped out of the shadows, grabbing Janet around the throat and holding a revolver to her head. "Drop the gun," he ordered. Immediately, Frank tossed down his revolver.

"I must congratulate you, Frank," Ed Kemble said. "That was fine deductive reasoning. Have you any more points to add?"

"Just one," Frank told him solemnly. "The clinching point. When you and Janet performed the fall from the building, you heard us shouting and knew that we were on to the fact that the stunt had been sabotaged.

"So in midair, you came up with a master stroke. To divert any suspicion away from yourself, you saved Janet. You were almost perfect."

"Almost?" Kemble asked, somewhat hurt.

"Yes," Frank insisted. "Only someone who knew that her air bag had been deflated would have thought to draw Janet over to the safe one."

Joe's eyes lit up. "Right! I was too busy admiring the old hero here to realize that."

"Old?" Ed Kemble gritted his teeth. "You'll regret that remark."

Ed ordered Gil Driscoll to untangle the support ropes. Then he told Wesley and Ty to complete the robbery. The henchmen got back to work. Before long, they swung back over the railing with a sack of jewels.

Ed took the goods from the bag and examined them carefully.

"Beautiful," he marveled. "Absolutely exquisite. And far more valuable than those gems we forfeited at the Garfield place."

He ordered Frank and Joe to walk ahead of him up another flight of stairs. From the top floor, the thieves directed them to an outdoor balcony.

Joe looked down and gulped. The balcony jutted out from the side of the mansion, directly overlooking the cliff. It was a long fall to the hard rocks and raging surf below.

Janet screamed as Ed Kemble pushed her hard against the low railing. Joe reached out and grabbed her just before she fell over.

Ed and Driscoll spread out to cover the three young people with their guns.

"It's such a shame that we'll have to sacrifice a few of the less precious gems." Kemble tossed a few of the valuables to Frank and Joe.

"But it's all part of my brilliant new plan," the actor assured them. "Since the police already believe that you're jewel thieves, we're going to provide them with more proof."

"At the same time taking the blame off yourselves," Frank growled.

"My thought exactly." Kemble grinned. "Tomorrow when the robbery is discovered, the police will also find your bodies smashed against the rocks below. With the jewels in your pockets, it will appear that the three of you had an accident escaping from your second heist. What's more, the rest of the jewels will never have to be accounted for, because everyone will believe they were washed out to sea."

Ty and Wesley arrived behind the other two crooks. Ed Kemble turned and gave them his famous movie star smile.

"Okay, here's our final stunt," he said. "Throw them over!"

Chapter

17

FRANK AND JOE stepped forward, shielding Janet from the stuntmen's assault. They locked arms, forcing Driscoll, Wesley, and Ty to take them on together.

The three thieves charged straight ahead, lowering their shoulders as they barreled into the Hardys. Frank and Joe took the force of the blow but still found themselves pushed back. Only the support of the railing prevented them from falling into the sea.

"Where do you think you're going?" Ed Kemble asked Janet.

The stunt girl ducked down and squirmed out from beneath Wesley's arm.

Ed grabbed her by the shoulder as she ran for the door. He dragged her back, bending her slim body over the rail. Relentlessly, Janet kicked and punched at Ed. But he was too strong for her.

"Help!" she screamed.

Joe turned just as Janet slid completely over the balcony. She was gone!

He went wild, hurling himself at the henchmen. A fist slammed into Wesley's jaw sent him reeling, while a snap kick to Ty's stomach left him moaning in pain.

Joe stumbled over them to the railing. Janet wasn't dead! With the last of her strength, she clung to the bottom of the balcony. Her feet dangled helplessly in the air.

Ed Kemble laughed as he brought his foot down on her fingers, taunting her as he applied more pressure.

Joe grabbed the movie star and flung him around like a rag doll. Suddenly it was Ed Kemble who was struggling not to fall into the sea. Joe was on him, his hands around Kemble's throat.

Janet lifted herself back onto the terrace.

"Joe, stop!" Janet shouted. "You'll kill him."

Slowly Joe's grip slackened, and he pulled Ed Kemble to his feet. The old star just stood there, smiling at him. Joe was puzzled. But when he turned around, he realized what made Kemble so happy.

Driscoll, Wesley, and Ty had Frank by the arms and legs. They swung him back and forth, ready to toss him out to sea. Frank struggled but, held tight by his limbs, was unable to break free.

One last time they swung Frank back, counting out loud as they prepared to send him flying over the rail.

"One—two—"

"Hold it right there!"

Suddenly the balcony was ablaze in light. Several spotlights shone brightly in the thieves' faces. Covering their eyes, they dropped Frank to the floor. Quickly he joined Joe and Janet.

Down below, four police cars had appeared on the cliff path. Through a bullhorn, Archie Fraser instructed the stuntmen to drop their weapons and give themselves up.

Ed Kemble stared astonished. His jaw hung open.

"But I don't understand," he mumbled. "How could the police possibly know we were here?"

With a slight grin, Frank slowly removed a piece of wire from his shirt pocket. He dangled it before Ed's eyes.

"I found this on the top of the doorway," he said casually, "and I thought you might want it back."

Kemble gritted his teeth. "You set off the silent alarm!"

The police continued to shout up through the bullhorn, telling the stuntmen to give themselves up. But Kemble didn't drop his weapon. Instead, he turned his gun on Frank.

"If I'm to be captured," Kemble said, "at least I can get my revenge on you."

Shielding his eyes from the glaring lights, he cocked his gun and aimed at Frank's chest.

A shot rang out, and Frank's body hurtled back against the rail!

"No!" Joe went for his brother, then turned to Kemble with murder in his eyes.

"Don't sweat it." Frank sat up. "I jumped back by reflex, but that wasn't Kemble's gun."

Turning to Kemble, they saw the old star tightly clasping a wounded wrist. His gun lay beside him on the floor.

Frank grinned. "Good shooting, Dad."

Fenton Hardy stepped onto the balcony, a smoking gun in his hand. "Chief Fraser let me lead the arrest squad into the mansion," he said. "Looks like we arrived just in time."

He smiled at Frank, Joe, and Janet. "Are all of you okay?"

"We are now," Joe replied.

The police disarmed Driscoll and the henchmen, locking handcuffs onto their wrists and reading them their rights.

"I flew cross-country as soon as I got your message," Fenton Hardy explained.

He turned and glared at Ed Kemble.

"But out in Hollywood," Fenton continued, "most of the pieces had begun to come together. Financial reports revealed that Kemble was broke. He lived high on the hog, and gambled most of his money away. In fact, he had to make this film without pay because he was so badly in debt to the producers. Isn't that right, Ed?"

Kemble hung his head. "I couldn't even get a role on a television show. Imagine, *me,* Ed Kemble, unable even to work on TV."

He clenched his fists. "Well, I was going to show them. At the same time as I was destroying their movie, I was going to steal enough money to pay off my debts and retire."

"It almost worked," Frank said, nodding. "Your sabotage shifted our attention from your real plans—for the robbery."

"Yes." Kemble nodded bitterly. "If it hadn't been for these two . . . apprentices, I would be rich beyond my wildest dreams."

As the police began to bring the thieves down to the awaiting patrol cars, Chief Archie Fraser came onto the balcony. He held out his hand to shake with Frank and Joe.

"I knew all along you two weren't criminals," Fraser said by way of an apology. "I just had to keep you guys on a string, to make sure you didn't get hurt."

"You did a fine job of acting, Chief," Joe told him straight-faced as he shook Fraser's hand. "Maybe they can use you in the movie."

"What movie?" Slowly in a daze of disbelief, Sy Osserman made his way onto the balcony. His mouth opened but no words came out—just a few whimpers.

"I got your message to meet you here, Chief."

He stared at Ed Kemble. "Don't tell me *he's* the saboteur. You can't arrest one of my stars. It will ruin my picture."

Fraser shook his head. "This time I can't oblige you, Mr. Osserman. We caught Kemble and the others in the act of attempted murder."

"Attempted murder?" The director's voice rose. "Well, in that case—" Slowly Osserman fumbled around in his coat pocket. "I have something for you, Chief. Thinking about it, I remembered that Frank and Joe were right. They had given me this reel of film after all. It had completely slipped my mind."

Joe gave him a squinty-eyed look. "I'll bet it did!"

He pointed an accusing finger at the director. "You were perfectly willing to have us rot in jail!"

Fenton Hardy abruptly stopped smiling. "Is that true, Mr. Osserman?"

Sheepishly, the director looked around. "Chill out, you guys. Of course I wasn't going to allow you to stay behind bars. It—it was merely a temporary arrangement—for your safety. Yeah, for your safety!"

Osserman slapped his forehead. "Only now, with Ed Kemble unable to work, I'm the one who's doomed."

"No, you're not," Frank told him.

"I'm not?"

"Think of the potential for publicity," Janet

chimed in. "I can see the headlines now. 'Stunt Apprentices Stump Stone-Stealing Star!' "

The director thought it over. Suddenly his face lit up and his disposition seemed to change before everyone's eyes.

"I like it," he said, nodding. "Come to think of it, most of Kemble's scenes are already in the can. With clever camerawork, and some new stunts—"

"You're forgetting one thing," Joe reminded him. "Gil, Wesley, and Ty are under arrest, and the captain is in the hospital. Frank and I are heading back home to Bayport now that the case is complete—you don't have a stunt team anymore."

Osserman uttered a cry of despair. "You're right! I'm finished!"

"Well, I have some good news." Archie Fraser cut into the conversation. "Especially for you, Janet. Ray Wynn has pulled out of his coma. The doctors called just before we left. In fact, they say he'll be up and around in no time."

Janet's eyes gleamed. She grinned, broke out in a wild whoop, and wrapped Archie Fraser in a bearhug, practically bowling the fat police chief over.

"Good news?" she yelled. "That's *great* news!"

Suddenly Sy Osserman stepped forward. "And I have a great idea! The captain might not be able to perform yet, but he can still conceive new stunts. As always, Janet can do Kitt Macklin's stunts, and—'' The director reached out and grabbed Frank and Joe by the arms. "If you two stay on for the rest of the summer, not as under-cover types, but as full-fledged stuntmen, we can complete the picture.''

Frank and Joe looked at each other. Then they turned to Janet.

"I'm game if you guys are," she said with a smile.

Frank grinned. "What do you say, Joe?"

Joe shook his head and threw up his arms.

"Why not?" he said, laughing. "It can't be any more dangerous than real life."

Frank and Joe's next case:

A student-exchange program brings the Hardys to sun-kissed Greece. But the moment they hit the scenic port of Piraeus, they land in deep trouble. What starts as a street fight soon escalates to a hornet's nest of espionage, kidnapping, and diplomatic double-cross.

Near Yugoslavia, Frank and Joe find themselves on a mission to rescue someone they don't know, for a cause they barely understand. Only one thing is certain—if the brother team fails this border run, they'll be ancient history . . . in *The Borderline Case,* Case #25 in The Hardy Boys Casefiles™.